SIMON SPOTLIGHT

An imprint of Simon & Schuster Children's Publishing Division ★ 1230 Avenue of the Americas, New York, New York 10020 ★ Copyright © 2011 by Simon & Schuster, Inc.

All rights reserved, including the right of reproduction in whole or in part in any form.

SIMON SPOTLIGHT and colophon are registered trademarks of Simon & Schuster, Inc.

Text by Alexis Barad-Cutler

Designed by Giuseppe Castellano

For information about special discounts for bulk purchases, please contact Simon & Schuster Special Sales at 1-866-506-1949 or business@simonandschuster.com.

Manufactured in the United States of America 0611 OFF

First Edition 10 9 8 7 6 5 4 3 2 1

ISBN 978-1-4424-2239-1 (pbk)

ISBN 978-1-4424-2240-7 (eBook)

Library of Congress Catalog Card Number 2011924449

**Monday.**

After Grizzly pr... locker room

**Spirit Level:**

Ready and (sort of) OK!

The gym at Port Angeles School was even noisier than usual this afternoon when I met up with my cheer co-captain, Jacqueline Sawyer, to lug the boxes that had arrived at my house earlier this morning over to the rowdy group of cheerleaders in their designated corner. I couldn't wait to show the Titans the new uniforms I designed for their team—for **REALZ** this time. Well, I mean, I **DID** design them the last time—it's just that there was an itsy-bitsy mix-up when Jacqui submitted the designs to the uniform company. See, she kinda put her own spin on them so that when the Titans got their new uniforms, instead of saying "Titans" on the shirts, it read "Tight Ends." This was Jacqui's way of getting back at her old teammates for kicking her off the squad, but it also put me in a totally awkward position.

GIVE ME A !!

Here's what the uniforms looked like when I first handed the sketch over to Jacqui.

"new" "titans uniform"

TITANS

TIGHT ENDS

ugh...

Jacqui's revenge!

And here's what they looked like after Jacqui had her revenge.

Ridiculous!! It looked like a football uniform married a cheerleader uniform and then had a baby uniform that went onto the discount rack at Filene's Basement. Total fashion faux pas.

Anyway, I made good on my promise to get the uniforms right this time, and thankfully, Jacqui stayed out of my way. Well, the truth is, she's back to (kinda) being friends again with Katie Parker, Titan head

GIVE ME A 2!

cheerleader and all-around Miss Perfect.

"Watch out, Grizzlies coming through!" cried Hilary Cho when she spotted us. Then she did a little roar, like a bear. Ha-ha. Get it? Grizzly Bears? Like I haven't heard that one before.

So, Hilary is the third girl in what my friends and I like to call the "Triumvirate" of the Titan cheerleaders: Katie Parker, Clementine Prescott, and Hilary Cho. Hilary pretty much just goes along with whatever Katie and Clementine think is cool. She's a total sheep. Baa, baa.

I hate it when the Titans get all snotty like that. I mean, the Grizzly Bears are cheerleaders too! OK, so we're kind of at the bottom of the cheerleading food chain. We don't, you know, walk down the hall strutting our killer abs and supershort skirts. And until just recently, we were living in uniforms from, like, twenty years ago. Gross! We're not friends with the football jocks (so annoying) and we don't have prime real estate in the cafeteria

old grizzlie uniform

GRIZZLIES

poop

GIVE ME A 3!

(Ha! We're lucky if we have a table at all). See map of caf.

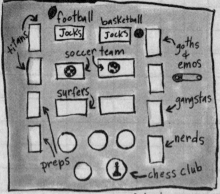

map of our cafeteria

Some might say we don't do or have those things because we are, like, so **ABOVE** that. Really? We don't because we can't. We're the B-team. The Grizzlies were formed because the school felt that no one should be turned away from wanting to participate in school-spirit-related activities. Anyone who doesn't make the cut for Titan tryouts automatically gets to be on the Grizzly squad. Hooray! So that's where we come in: We are the voice of the uncoordinated. We also come in handy when the Titans are so busy competing to get to Nationals that they can't cheer at our school's games. I mean, who else would cheer for debate team, chess club, or math league?

But still, there's no need for people like Hilary to rub it in our faces.

GIVE ME A 4!

I'm far from uncoordinated, but I know I'm not quite Nationals material. Still I'm a way better cheerleader than anyone on my team (except for Jacqui, obvs, but she WAS a Titan once, after all). My ultimate dream is to be a Titan. I just keep hoping that if I practice harder, learn the Titans' killer choreography, and hit every stunt, I'll be good enough to wear one of the uniforms I worked so hard designing for their squad.

It would be nice if I had more time to work on my clothing designs, though. Sometimes it feels sort of like an obsession. When I'm not sketching out new stunts for my team in this here journal, I'm pretty much designing clothes (and cheer outfits).

my never-leave-the-house-
without-it journal

"So, what's with the boxes?" asked Clementine, Triumvirate member #2. "Make it quick. We're bugging out." (Ugh. Being on Clementine's bad side is never a good idea. Ever. She can cut you with just one nasty look, seriously. Once, she looked at a seventh grader funny and the girl broke out in hives!! For realz.)

I explained that I was about to present her and her team with new uniforms. Of course this got Clementine's attention. (Anything having to do with

GIVE ME A
5!

Clementine usually does.) She knelt down beside the box I'd opened to grab one of the plastic-wrapped uniforms.

"Huh, this doesn't look like a disaster," she said, checking out the skirt appreciatively. This was a high compliment coming from Clementine. She smoothed the skirt against her spray-tanned legs. "Ooh, and it's short, too!"

I could just see her thinking about how great it will look on her when she prances down the halls of Port Angeles (as if she needs **MORE** guys looking in her direction).

Jacqui started opening another box just as Katie came over to us looking flustered.

"Oh, good! The uniforms!" she said, tightening her ponytail nervously. "Hey, thanks, Madison. We've got to make this quick, though. We're starting to get ready for the Regional Qualifier today."

Sigh. The Regional Qualifier. As soon as she breathed those words, I had this insane feeling of jealousy. Which I **HATE**. But I would kill to be in one of those competitions. The Regional Qualifier is, like, one of **THE** most important ones of the year. If your team places in it, then you get to go on to the Regional Championships. Without qualifying for Regionals? You can kiss Nationals (i.e., the holy grail of cheer

GIVE ME A 6!

competitions) good-bye.

"These are amazing!" squealed Katie, holding a uniform out in front of her. "OMG, Madison. Loves!"

She was literally smiling from ear to ear. Jacqui gave me a little wink.

"Awesome. Glad you guys like 'em," I said.

T.G. I'm **BEYOND** relieved. I mean, can you even imagine what would've happened if she'd, like, hated them? I couldn't mess up **AGAIN**!! Not with my future team captain (fingers crossed! ☺). Also, Katie and I have become more friendly just recently. I bet if I hadn't made these uniforms look perfect, she would've gone right back to ignoring me. No, thank you!

"Hey, Coach!" shouted Clementine. "Look!" She pointed to the boxes of uniforms.

Coach Whipley glanced in our direction, then gave Clementine the thumbs-up. (Obviously uniforms aren't a big deal to her. Hmph!) Then she started barking orders about permission slips and choosing roommates for the overnight stay at the competition site. Jacqui and I took that as our cue to leave and headed over to the Grizzly corner of the gym.

As we walked to our mat to start stretching I asked Jacqui if the Titans always get this freaked before big competitions.

GIVE ME A 7!

"Well, the Titans don't take any competition lightly," she said with a laugh. "But I heard that this year a lot of schools are nervous about the qualifier because the judges are supposed to be pickier than ever."

"Hmm," I said, starting on some neck rolls. "So, how often are the rumors true?"

Jacqui looked off beyond the bleachers behind me, thinking. "Um, well, last year there was a rumor that teams would be judged superharshly on their dance routines, and in the end even the best dancers didn't place as well as they usually do. So . . ." she shrugged.

"Do you think the Titans really have anything to worry about?" I asked.

"Yeah," said Jacqui. "They don't have me on the team anymore." She laughed. "No, but seriously, even though they freak out, they always place."

Just then my mom—I mean, Coach Carolyn—walked into the gym, followed by the rest of my teammates. Sometimes I wonder how I got so "lucky" (yeah, right) that I get to hang with Mom not only at home, but at school, too. To what do I owe this honor?! I'm just glad she didn't get an office here. That would have been **THE END**. I feel bad thinking this, but sometimes I wish my mom was more normal. Normal moms probably can't say that they were homecoming queens, prom

GIVE ME AN 8!

queens, cheerleading captains—basically every popular title a person can have. And it's hard to be on the loser cheerleading team knowing that Mom's cheer skills were legendary at my school. So when Jacqui convinced me that Mom should be the Grizzly coach, it was

My Mom's Legacy

pretty rough. At first, all Mom could talk about was cheer, cheer, cheer. Oh, AND she was constantly butting in about Grizzly stuff that wasn't really her problem. But ever since we had a big talk about it, I think it's working out pretty well. Except for when she calls me "sweetie" at practice.

"Hey, sweetie," said Mom, ruffling my hair when she walked past me.

Grrr.

"Hi, sweeeetie!" teased Matt Herrington, one of the two ex-football-jocks on our squad.

Ian McClusky, his partner in crime, chuckled behind him.

I gave them both a dirty look. I think Matt and Ian might actually have some cheer potential, even though

GIVE ME A 9!

they're total clowns. Their upper-body strength would make them really good bases for partner stunts—that is, if they didn't get hysterical every time they had to lift one of us girls. Morons.

"As captains, you know we can easily make you do, like, a hundred push-ups just for disrespecting us," said Jacqui. This seemed to quiet them down.

I started the team on our usual warm-up—some good stretches on the mat for our calves, hips, and hamstrings—and then back bends.

"Help! Help!" someone squeaked. Tabitha Sue Stevens, of course. She was trying to get out of the stretch but had managed to get her neck into an awkward position. I went over to disentangle her from, um, herself. Tabitha Sue is one of my secret fave squad members because she'll try anything at least once even if she's terrified. She has the most spirit on the whole team—which annoys Jared Handler to no end since he would like to think he wins at being the most into the Grizzlies and into, well, everything cheer related. And Tabitha Sue always smiles after she falls. I placed my hand under the small of her back and helped her ease out of the stretch.

"Thanks, Madison," she said, wiping small beads of sweat from her forehead.

GIVE ME A 10!

"You got it," I said. "Watch me do this one more time, and I'll spot you next time, ok?"

During a break I told the team about the Titans going to the Regional Qualifier.

"Is zis competitive vat you call 'beeg'?" asked Katarina Tarasov in her typical botched-up version of the English language. I heart Katarina a ton because she's got mad gymnastics skillz, which definitely helps bring the Grizzlies up a notch.

"Yeah, it's one of the bigger competitions of the season," my mom said. "It determines whether they'll go to Regionals. I can guarantee you'll be seeing the Titans work even harder than normal for the next few weeks." She nodded to the corner of the gym where the Titans were practicing their perfect-looking jumps.

"I've never seen the Titans in, like, 'not cool' mode," said Matt. "They actually seem kind of nervous."

Jared squinted over at the cheerleaders. "No way—I don't believe it. I think the only thing that would make Hilary or Clementine nervous is if Sephora ran out of their favorite lip gloss color."

Ian muttered something under his breath, probably a dig at Jared.

"Oh, I'm thinking someone wants to do two hundred push-ups now," Jacqui said, looking directly at Ian.

GIVE ME AN
III!

Ian mimed a halo over his head with his index finger and smiled angelically.

"Ok, guys, rest time is over," I told them. "If you ever want to get your jumps to look like theirs, then partner up."

Everyone groaned because they knew what was coming. I had each person take turns putting his or her ankle on another person's shoulder and having the other person go from a squatting position to standing until the person stretching couldn't take it anymore. Jacqui and I have been doing this stretch for years— but the rest of the Grizzlies will never get their legs as high as ours if they don't take their stretching to the next level.

I saw that Mom was watching us practice, but she had a funny look on her face—like she was totally thinking about something else. Then it hit me! I know that look. It's the look she has whenever she has something brutal in mind for me—or in this case, the Grizzlies. Something is brewing in Mom Brain. Why do I have a feeling it's not going to be pretty?

GIVE ME A
12!

# Monday, November 15

## Spirit Level:
Cupies Before Cuties

yes!

no!

Tonight Mom was überquiet all through dinner. Too quiet. And she had that same weird expression on her face from earlier at practice. Again, **NOT** a good sign.

"All right. What are you thinking? Spit it," I said, trying to smile even though I was only half joking.

She swallowed a sip of her skim milk and announced brightly, "The Grizzlies are going with the Titans to the Regional Qualifier." Then she stuck her fork into a meatball and crossed her arms over her chest as if to say, "And that's final!"

My jaw almost fell into my spaghetti. The Grizzlies? At the qualifier? Uh, did she drink some crazy with her milk? The Grizzlies

tall glass of crazy juice

GIVE ME A 13!

don't even cheer at real games. The squad can't even do back tucks. No, scratch that—they can't even do back walkovers! How did she think all of a sudden we would be good enough to compete at something like the Regional Qualifier?

"Honey, relax. I didn't mean the Grizzlies would be competing!" she said, reading my mind.

I let out a breath of relief.

"I meant that I think it would be a great idea for the Grizzlies to go along with the Titans and witness what a real competition is like," Mom continued. "I remember the feeling of walking into one of the big competitions. The drama, the crowds, seeing all the other schools . . ." Mom's eyes were wide with excitement, the way they get when she cartwheels down memory lane.

"Yeah," I said. "I've read about how crazy those competitions can get. I'd actually love to see one up close and personal."

Ok, so Mom and I agreeing on something cheer related? This has **NOT** been happening a lot lately. We should've taken a snapshot of that moment and put it in a frame for Maddy Alley. Sure, it

GIVE ME A 14!

would've looked a little out of place next to all the pics of me in my dance and gymnastics uniforms through the years. But still, when I think about how much Mom and I were fighting just a month ago, it's kind of a big deal when we think like a team about cheerleading.

"I'm going to talk to Principal Gershon and see what we can do," said Mom. "I think it will be good for the squad, you know? They'll be able to see why we work them so hard—and also see that competing isn't just cute dances and fun tricks."

"Oh, Mom, don't crush Jared's dreams," I said. (Mean joke, I know.)

I wonder how the Grizzlies will react to seeing a Regional Qualifier up close. . . . We only really get to see the Titans show off at home games, which is intimidating enough. I can just imagine what the team will think when they see other squads like the Titans—or better—all in one place, with music blasting and no sports teams to distract us from the spectacle. The Grizzlies are going to be psyched when they hear about this. It'll probably help get the squad more pumped about all the tough stuff we've been practicing lately. And excuse me, but who doesn't L—O—V—E a field trip?

After I did the dishes, I went up to my room and

GIVE ME A
15!

signed on to video chat.

Evan was online, and he started giving me a hard time as usual.

"All's well in cheer world, I hear?" he asked. "Word on the street is that the new uniforms were a big hit."

I think Evan likes to pretend he looks down on cheerleaders, but really he's always up on the latest cheer news, sometimes even before I am. Scary. And every time a Titan cheerleader passes him in the hallway, he gets all tongue-tied and forgets which direction he was walking in. SUPERscary. And gross!

"News travels fast," I replied.

"Hilary was telling everyone after practice that the skirts were the perfect length to show off her 'supertoned quads,'" Evan said in his best ditzy cheerleader voice.

best guy friend ♡

could use a make over ☺

Kind of cute, if he wanted to be.

comic book obsessed!!

GIVE ME A 16!

"Sounds like a win-win," I joked. "Anyway, how did you hear about this?"

"I met up with a few kids after school to trade some SuperBoys for a vintage Plastic Man comic. And I listen and observe." He winked at the screen.

"How James Bond of you."

I could hear Evan's dad call his name and announce that it was time for dinner. "Gotta check you later," said Evan. "Time to grab some grub."

Just as I x-ed out of the chat screen, another chat window popped up.

Bevan Ramsey. The boy I totally heart with all my . . . well, heart. But all I could think was "ugh." Strange, I know. The thing is, a month ago my reaction to Bevan Ramsey texting or chatting me would have been to scream ecstatically, "You're joking!! Bevan Ramsey? Does he even know my name?"

Sometimes I like writing his name over and over (like so) just to see what it looks like. Even his name is, like, interesting and cool and different from the other guys' at our school. Kind of perfect. Just like him. Sigh.

GIVE ME A 17!

I still can't believe that Bevan—the same guy I've been dreaming about for months—actually asked me out on a date after the last soccer game. (Like, on a real date—not one that happens only in my dreams, and NOT like a study date. An actual, full-fledged "can we check out a movie or something" kind of date.) I almost died, I was so happy. Actually, to be totally honest, I was doing double herkies of joy in my head. It's too bad that five seconds after I said yes I realized to my own horror that if I ever want to be a Titan, I can't go near Bevan with a ten-foot pole. Katie will KILL me if I start dating her ex-boyfriend. I wish Jacqui had never told me about Katie's stupid

The Perfection that is BEVAN Ramsey!

wavy hair

amazing shoulder muscles

drool-worthy abs

espresso colored eyes!

new cheer move by madison hays: The Bevan Ramsey herkie of joy!

GIVE ME AN 18!

no-dating-cheerleader-exes rule! It sucks because I really, really, **REALLY** like him. But as they say in cheer, cupies before cuties.

Shoe Shopping!

Luckily, after he asked me out, Bevan went on vacay with his fam for a whole week. But since he's been back, avoiding him has been **REALLY** hard. We didn't decide on an exact day for our "big night out," so I figure that as long as he can't talk to me, I'll never have to **FORMALLY** turn him down. Good plan, huh?? Lanie's even helped me escape from his gorgeous clutches a couple of times.

If we would see him coming toward me in the hall, she'd put a really serious look on her face and then shout the words "shoe shopping" to make sure he wouldn't want to interrupt our "girl talk." And yesterday, in the lunch line in the caf, she saw him just about to tap my shoulder so she shouted, "Mads! Help! There's a fly in my tuna!"

"Maddy. Ummmmmm. U there?" he wrote.

For some reason, I didn't think he would go to the effort of actually trying to contact me outside of school . . . but looky look, there he was. Double ugh.

GIVE ME A 19!

Well, at that point it was too late. He already saw I was online, so it would have been completely loser-y of me to just ignore him. It took me, like, ten years, but I finally clicked the "accept" button on the screen. Then I held my breath and freaked out about what I would say if he mentioned our date.

"Present LOL! Yep, here. What's up?" I typed back.

"I'm starting 2 think I need 2 change my deodorant," Bevan typed.

"Ahahah, yep, u smell 🙂," I wrote back finally.

"Where u been?" he typed.

Ummmm. Avoiding you? It's a fun game we play. Aren't you having fun??? Grrr.

"Just around. Lots of Grizzlies stuff going on."

"Yeah?"

"Yep. But I can't really chat now, either. Dinnertime," I typed.

I cringed. He must think I'm the weirdest person alive. One minute (or one week) ago I was practically speechless in his presence. The next I'm all, "Yeah. Soooo busy. Ya know. Things to do." Like I'm so cool.

"K. u busy tom?" he wrote.

### AHHHHHHH!

"Yah, unforch. Big day @ practice." (Which was kinda true.) "Grizzlies r going w Titans 2 Regionals!"

GIVE ME A 20!

"Nice!!!"

"I gotta go tho ☹."

"Kkk talk 2 u l8r."

I signed off chat as fast as possible. How much longer will I be able to keep this whole hiding-from-Bevan thing going? How do you avoid the cutest guy in school—especially when he's practically chasing you down? (Especially when it's so COMPLETELY amazing that he's chasing you, and instead of avoiding it, you'd much rather be screaming it from the mountaintops???!!) Ok. I need to stop stressing about this. But sometimes life is so unfair!!!

GIVE ME A 2!!

# Tuesday, November 16

sleepy time, under the covers

# Spirit ~~Level~~ Rule #11

set Goals and Accomplish Them

Ruh-roh! Never a dull moment in Grizzly World. At the beginning of practice, Mom told everyone about how she had gotten permission from the school for our team to go along to the Regional Qualifier with the Titans.

"You know how important I think it is for you guys to observe amazing routines and stunts so you can aspire to do them yourselves," said Mom, pacing in front of us during our stretches. "And until now, you've mainly only gotten to see the Titans on their home court. This upcoming competition is pretty major." She looked each one of us in the eye. "We're going to go there, support our fellow cheerleaders, and also learn about what it takes to compete against awesome cheerleaders from all over our area. And it will be fun!" She pumped a fist in the air.

GIVE ME A 22!

Ian raised his hand and waved it around. "Um, Coach Carolyn?"

"Ian, we're not in a classroom. But yes?"

"I think it's really cool that you planned this trip for us and everything. But what does this trip actually have to do with us? Like, what's in it for the Grizzlies?"

I could tell my mom was surprised by his bad attitude. She's not used to people who are all about themselves. Carolyn Hays's middle name is Teamwork. I think that's what made her such a good cheerleader back in the day. Well, that and her ridiculous flexibility and flyer skills.

"Well, you're going to get to see what a real competition is like," replied Mom. "Aren't you tired of watching Bring It On on TV? Now you can see it for real!"

Unfortunately, no one was buying into Mom's enthusiasm.

"A trip is fine, but what I want to know is, when do we get to cheer at another, like, soccer game? Or better, a basketball game!" said Matt.

"Yeah!" said Ian, giving Matt a high five.

Jacqui and I exchanged troubled looks. What had gotten into everyone?

GIVE ME A
23!

Katarina, who had bent herself into a very uncomfortable-looking pretzel, agreed with Ian and Matt. "Yeah, ve vant competitive too. Vy aren't ve making zee competing?" she pouted. But it was kind of hard to be angry at her whining, with her legs all twisted behind her ears like that.

"Katarina, stop that—you look like that <u>Exorcist</u> girl," said Matt.

"Vat iz wrong vit being an exercise girl? I like exercise," said Katarina, missing the joke. Clearly she wasn't familiar with American horror movies.

Even Tabitha Sue giggled.

"Come on, guys, we'll get to cheer at another game soon," I said, trying to take the pressure off Mom.

"Really? When?" asked Jared, his hands on his hips.

"I—I—I don't know," I stammered. "Actually, I do," I lied. "When we're ready, which we're not . . . yet." I tried to smile confidently.

All through practice I couldn't stop thinking about how my teammates have a good point. They need some competition to keep their spirits up. Without a goal to achieve, what's the point in working so hard every day for hours after school? But for them to ever compete, they'll have to really get better. Not just be able to do some good cartwheels and layouts, but like, actually do

GIVE ME A 24!

some stunts. And if they do . . . maybe the Grizzlies can do a statewide cheer competition for small novice teams? That can't be that SO out of the question for us. One thing's for sure: The Grizzlies will never get better if their hearts aren't in the sport. So how could I raise everyone's spirits and at the same time make them better cheerleaders?

Blam! Suddenly it hit me. This old book called The Spirit Rules that I'd heard about. It's practically a Titan legacy handed down from cheerleader to cheerleader. The Spirit Rules is totally on the DL, but my mom told me

about it a while back and Jacqui even mentioned it a few weeks ago. Only Titans are allowed to own their own copies. But Jacqui once let it slip that a couple of years ago the Titans all got new editions and the school asked them to donate one of their older editions to our school library. They keep it hush-hush because they don't want other teams to find out about it.

So after practice I headed over to the library. The

last time I was in the library, I'd been researching the salem witch trials, but I doubted The Spirit Rules would be anywhere near the witch section. On the other hand, the title did have the word "Spirit" in it. . . .

Miss Doverly, the head librarian, is really pretty for a librarian. You totally wouldn't expect her to be working all alone with a bunch of dusty old books and overachieving kids. She kind of reminds me of Lanie, but without all the snark. I sometimes wonder if she's, like, secretly some kind of CIA agent and this is her cover.

"Hey, Miss Doverly? Where would I find nonfiction books about sports?"

She looked at me kind of like, "Hey, nice to see you round these parts." Guess I don't come to the library as often as I should. (Note to self: Frequenting the library would apparently make not only your father, but your librarian **VERY** happy.) She pointed me down a long hallway, then to the left and up some stairs. Basically, the no-man's-land of our library. I wonder if the janitor even bothers

Miss Doverly:
Head Librarian—
C.I.A. Agent

GIVE ME A 26!

vacuuming this area. The floor creaked with each step I took toward the "S" bookshelf.

I almost completely missed it at first. It was hidden in between two enormous books about skiing. Like, why would we need books about skiing in Port Angeles, Washington? I didn't even know what snow looked like until I was twelve and Dad took me to Colorado to learn how to snowboard (which, except for the free s'mores at the lodge, was an absolute disaster). The copyright page of The Spirit Rules was ripped out and the pages were a bit yellowed—it looked like it was first printed back when Mom was a Titan. The jacket even had our school colors: red, white, and blue. I

opened it to a random page and saw a drawing of one of the famous Titan double Swedish falls pyramids. This must be where they learned some of their original tricks! There's a chapter called "Making the Team," which is all about what skills you need before even considering trying to become a cheerleader. As I read it I was thinking, "OMG! Some of these tips will probably help the Grizzlies a ton!" Another chapter called "Not

GIVE ME A 27!

So Routine!" breaks down the basics of what a good routine has in it and what judges usually look for at competitions. In each chapter there are different "spirit rules," like "Set Goals and Accomplish Them." No wonder the Titans live for this book (and they say cheerleaders don't study!). Even though it's practically ancient (sorry, Mom, but twenty years ago is totally ancient history nowadays . . .), The Spirit Rules has it all. I was dying to get home, crash onto my bed, and tear through this book so I could start using it to the team's advantage. If The Spirit Rules can't help my team's attitude problem, nothing can.

When I went to check out the book, Miss Doverly looked at it appreciatively. Weird.

"Ah, yes," she said, taking out the Port Angeles library card inside and stamping it with a due date. "Haven't seen this one taken out in a while. Or maybe—" she went to look at the last date the book had been checked out, and I saw that there actually wasn't a date there. Heh. Guess the Titans do a good job of keeping the book a secret.

"Well, the Titans have their own copy," I said. "So I doubt they would check this one out."

"That makes you the first Grizzly to see it, then, right?" she winked.

GIVE ME A
28!

Which was kind of cool. A) She actually knows I'm a Grizzly! B) She knows who the Grizzlies are! Maybe if the Grizzlies get a dose of the advice the Titans have been following since forever, we'll become a bit more like the Titans in other ways.

I quickly texted Jacqui: "Got sumthin to show u tom."

"What???" she texted back.

"A surprise. But u will likkkke it!"

"K. Excited!"

At home the kitchen smelled like lemons and fried bread crumbs. Yum—chicken cutlets! After I set the table, I showed Mom my big find.

"Where did you get this?" Mom said with wonder in her voice, touching the worn paper delicately.

"There's this magical, secret place that cheerleaders hardly ever go. It's called the li-bra-ry," I joked.

Mom laughed. "What I mean is, this book was a big Titan secret when I was a cheerleader. And I didn't realize that it was actually available to the masses."

"Do you think it can help us?" I asked, chewing my lip nervously. I served myself some salad and waited for her to answer.

"I <u>am</u> worried a bit about what everyone said today.

GIVE ME A 29!

I thought they'd be excited about the trip. But I guess becoming better at the sport isn't enough for them." She lowered her sea-foam-colored eyes from my gaze. For a moment, she looked really sad. Sometimes I forget how much the Grizzlies mean to her.

"Yeah, I didn't realize the team was so unhappy either," I agreed. Then I thought about one of the rules that I read in the book when I was looking through it in the library. "I think we need to give them a goal."

"You know, I think you're onto something, Madison. Let's think about it. A goal for the Grizzlies!" she singsonged. "Has a nice ring to it, doesn't it?"

Ok, so she took it too far with that, as usual. She's probably picturing it on T-shirts by now.

LAME! But already I could tell that Mom's mood was getting brighter. She loves nothing more than turning the wheels in her head around and around on something cheer related.

Before I went up to my room, she lightly touched my arm. "I'm proud of you, Madington. You're

A GOAL
for the
Grizzlies

too FAR, mom.

GIVE ME A 30!

showing real initiative, trying to find a creative way to solve your team's problem." She nodded toward the book in my hands. "And that book is a great start."

Later on I called Lanes.

"You? At the library?" she asked. "Were they having a cheer bake sale?"

"Um, excuse you, no," I huffed. "I was checking out a book."

"Let me guess. It has something to do with cheerleading or fashion design?"

"Wow, Lanes, give me zero credit for my intellectual interests, why don't you? But, actually, yeah," I admitted. "It is a cheer book. But it's really cool! It's just what Jacqui and I need to get our team hyped about, you know, cheering at the uncoolest games on the planet."

"Yeah, I can see that."

"And also, it will make the team even more excited about cheering on the Titans at the Regional Qualifier we're going to at the end of the month. Which—Ohmigod! I didn't even tell you about it yet!"

"Wait—you guys are going to go with the Titans? Like, on one of their overnight competitions? Whoa. That's a pretty big deal."

"Well, you know my mom and her 'watch and learn'

GIVE ME A 3!!

policy. She wants us to see what a real competition is like."

"Does that mean more SuperBoy fund-raising for Evan and me?" asked Lanie, a slight sense of dread in her voice. I can't blame her for being worried—it was a **TON** of work for her and Evan last time around.

"Nah, we're gonna go the old-fashioned route, like a car wash or bake sale. We need to involve the team more in the fund-raising. Again, the whole lack-of-spirit thing."

"Ah. Gotcha."

I didn't want to talk too long to Lanes because I have homework to do—as in, reading The Spirit Rules ☺. I also have **SCHOOL** homework to do . . . but in weighing my priorities, I think that can wait till tomorrow morning before class.

But before I can climb into my comfy pj's with the bunnies on them (so chic! JK), I **HAVE** to check my computer to see if Bevan tried to chat with me, even though I know it would be awkward. Because even if a girl isn't allowed to talk to the guy she likes, she's allowed to **WANT** him to want to talk to her, right? Grrr. No, that's not really fair, is it? I wonder what The Spirit Rules says about situations like this. Probably that I need to have a goal re: Bevan, just like

GIVE ME A 32!

I need to have one for the Grizzlies. Ok, so what's my goal when it comes to Bevan Ramsey? If I don't know what it is, how can I "accomplish it"?

Sigh. Just checked. No chat from Bevan.

Boo hoo.

GIVE ME A
33!

## Spirit Rule #2!

Know the Basics

Lanes came up to me first thing this morning before class and told me she had this "epiphany" after we spoke about the competition last night. I should have known this was not going to be good. The last time Lanie had an "epiphany" I ended up with a haircut that looked like a mullet and took me almost two years to grow back.

"Tell me everything you know about Regional Qualifier competitions," she said, matching my pace as I hurried to class. I'd just finished up the homework I'd put off doing the night before.

"Ok, now you have me bugging out," I said.

"I need to know," said Lanie, her hands on her hips.

GIVE ME A 34!

Seeing Lanie with her fishnet tights and fake, blue-streaked hair saying the word "Regional" made me want to laugh out loud. "Just <u>why</u> are you so excited about something related to cheer?"

"Since it makes the peeerrrfect story for my next article for the <u>Daily Angeles</u>!" Lanie declared proudly.

(Side note: The <u>Daily Angeles</u> is our school newspaper. It used to be really lame, but then Lanie signed up and took on a leadership role, switching out the boring articles with more exciting ones and adding new columns, like movie and music reviews, blogs to follow, and a special scandal section. Now it's actually kinda juicy . . . go, Lanie!!)

With all the stuff that's been going on in my life—the Grizzlies, the uniforms for the Titans, and Bevan—I completely forgot about Lanie's article. Awesome BFF I am! She's been agonizing for practically two weeks over what to write. She knew she wanted to do some kind of "exposé" but didn't know what to do it about.

We stopped right outside Room 302, where I had English in T minus two minutes.

"So, you want to do an exposé on cheerleading?"

I have to admit, I'm a little worried about this one.

"Not the way you think," said Lanie, raising her forefinger in protest. "I was doing some asking around,

GIVE ME A 35!

and I found out that the boys' lacrosse team wasn't allowed to go to last year's away sectionals game because the school said they didn't have the funding and the team couldn't raise enough money on their own."

"And?"

"And," Lanie said, dropping her voice to a whisper, "I also discovered that the amount of money that each sports team gets from Port Angeles isn't exactly what you call <u>even</u>." She waited for a few people to file past us into class before continuing. "Mads, the Titans are getting <u>way</u> more cashola than anyone else."

I've never really thought about this before. I mean, when I was upset about how the Titans always have the nicest, newest uniforms and the Grizzlies had, well, the grizzliest, grimiest uniforms, I just assumed it was because the school preferred the Titans over us. And I didn't really blame them. But I never imagined that the Titans were getting special treatment over EVERY sports team at school.

"So, your article is going to be about how the Titans don't deserve the amount of money they get from the school?" I know I must have been frowning when I said that. Even though they get a lot of moola from Port Angeles, it doesn't seem all that unfair. The Titans rock at every game and take home tons of trophies at

GIVE ME A 36!

competitions every year. Can our school's other teams say the same? Of course, this also means that teams like the Grizzlies get, well, nada . . . not even a paid coach. Which sorta ticks me off. So . . . I guess I'd have to say I'm torn on this one.

"Give me some credit, Mads. I'm an honest reporter. I'll do the research and show whether the Titans really deserve the extra dough. If they're really all that, then it will be obvious that they're worth the money." Lanie shrugged. "And now that you guys are going to the Regional Qualifier too, I can get even more juice."

"Juice?" I asked, raising my eyebrows. I really don't want her to say anything in the article that will put the Titans in a bad light.

"Info. The full scoop. The whole enchilada. So, will you help me? With the article?"

Ok, so Lanie is my best friend, and even though I have some small doubts about this, I have to just believe that she'll do a good job of reporting and be fair when she writes about the Titans . . . right? Besides, she'd kill me if I got all secretive about talking cheer stuff. Lanie and I don't keep secrets from each other.

"Duh, of course," I said, more brightly than I actually felt. "But I'm warning you: Once you get me talking cheerleading, it will be hard to stop." I hoisted my

GIVE ME A
37!

backpack onto my shoulder and turned to go into class.

"I'm counting on it." She smiled.

"See ya later."

Just as I turned to wave bye to her, I saw Bevan leaning against a locker across the hall. He was talking to a soccer friend. We locked eyes for a second, and he gave me the most adorable smile. I waved back dorkily—I'm talking full arm extending up into the air, swaying back and forth, like I was waving at someone departing on a ship. I'd really hoped this idiotic behavior would stop once he actually asked me out. Oh well. Anyway, that time I actually had a real reason I couldn't talk to him—I had to duck into class or I'd be late. If I'm really lucky, this might be my only Bevan run-in of the day. My fingers are crossed.

In other news, right before lunch I was finally able to do my "big reveal" to Jacqui. We met up by a group of unused lockers outside the caf. I slowly unzipped my backpack. "Are you ready?" I asked.

"You're killing me, Madison Hays," said Jacqui, tapping her foot. "Just what is so exciting that you had to keep it a secret, like, the whole day?"

"Ta-da!" I said, holding The Spirit Rules out in front of her.

It took a second for it to register, but then

GIVE ME A 38!

Jacqui smiled. "Hey! This is awesome! You know, we had a version of this book last year—I think Katie has it as cheer captain. But she never uses it, really. Once in a while she talks about looking at it for, like, the big problems, but I don't think she uses it like Titans did a long time ago. This is supposed to be the book of books on cheerleading."

"Yeah, that's what I heard," I said. "And you told me about it a couple weeks ago, remember?"

"Oh, right!" She hit herself on the forehead. "Guess I'm not the best at keeping secrets." She shrugged.

"It can't hurt to try out some of the tips—that's what I'm thinking," I said. "For example, one of the rules in the book is 'Always Set Goals and Accomplish Them.' I was talking to my mom last night, and I think we need to set a goal for the Grizzlies. Like, what about some kind of novice competition?"

Jacqui stared down at the book. "That's an awesome idea. That'll definitely give them something to work toward so they can stop all their whining."

I nodded. "Exactly—that's why I went looking for this book in the first place. I thought it could give me some ideas."

Jacqui closed her eyes, thinking. "We could do something for beginning cheerleaders. Why not?

GIVE ME A 39!

There's the Washington Get Up and Cheer competition at the end of the year. They take all levels and sizes of squads."

"Do you think we can even qualify as a level?" I asked, half joking.

"Who needs a dose of spirit <u>now</u>?" said Jacqui, shoving me in the side with the book.

"Ow! I was joking!" I said. "Sort of."

"All right, let's tell the team about it later. They'll love it. But we're gonna make them work for it."

"Totes," I agreed.

Hurrah! I love this plan ☺.

## AFTER PRACTICE, LOCKER ROOM

Man oh man. Of course I ran into Bevan again later today, right before practice, in front of the locker

rooms. And this time, I couldn't just duck into another class. Unless I wanted to pretend I'd gone crazy-pants and be like, "Oh, Mr. Hobart's class moved to the girls' locker room!"

"Hey, Madison. 'Sup?" he said. He was wearing those kneesocks that I heart so much.

My face turned beet red because that's just what happens when I'm around him.

"Hey, Bevan. Not much. You off to practice?" I couldn't believe I even asked that. Ring, ring! Hi, Maddy? Yes, this is Logic speaking. Of course he was off to practice. Why else would he

Bevan's socks = cuteness ♥

be in the gym, dressed like that? Piano lessons?

Loser!

Bevan looked down at his cleats.

"Yeah, I'm hitting the weights first with some of the guys. So . . . how was English class?"

ring
ring

"It was, um, English." I laughed. "We took turns reading from Hamlet, and Mr. Cooper yelled at us for not being 'emotive' enough. Then Evan was texting me lines from the play mixed together with popular movie lines and had me cracking up."

"I bet now Mr. Cooper thinks he has a great sense of humor," said Bevan.

"Either that, or he thinks I was delirious. Take your pick." I felt myself getting less nervous, thank

GIVE ME A 4!!

goodness. But then I remembered—ahhh!—our date. He was probably going to ask about it. And then what would I say?

"You want to hang out after practice tonight?"

**OMG, OMG, OMG.** This wasn't the way things were supposed to go. What about our **PLANNED** date? Was **THIS** the date? I thought I'd have a chance to say no to, like, a specific time and day. I didn't think he would ask me to just "hang out" after practice—which gave me no time to think of an excuse. "Quick, Mads," I was saying to myself. "Think of something!!"

"Uh, um . . . I . . ."

Bevan smiled halfheartedly. "Hey, it's cool. If you're busy, whatever." He turned around to head toward the weight room.

"It's just that—that—," I stammered. And then I burst out with the first thing that came into my head: "Jacqui and I have to plan this car wash thing after practice."

It was actually kind of true. We did have to plan our car wash—and soon. Which meant Jacqui and I would need to talk about it. But as soon as I said it, I realized it sounded lame. A car wash?! Like any girl in Port Angeles School would choose a car-wash-planning

GIVE ME A 42!

session over a date with Bevan Ramsey.

He nodded, looking a little surprised, and started to walk away. He didn't even turn around as he shouted, "Maybe another time!"

Even though this is the right thing to do—to not go out with Bevan because it will make Katie mad with the fury of a thousand suns (or so I've been told)—I didn't mean to hurt his feelings. I mean, I knew it would crush **ME** into billions of pieces, but that I can handle. The thing is, I didn't think it would turn out like this! He seemed really sad when I said no. And the fact that he didn't turn around when I tried to talk to him—that kind of hurt **MY** feelings! Gah! I am so confused. Is making Katie happy really worth hurting someone else—and myself—in the process? New goal for moi: Figure out who I want to hurt less, me, Bevan, or Katie.

Even though the Bevan sitch was (and still is!) unresolved, I vowed to put it behind me during practice. My teammates needed me to be on my game. It was time to introduce them to Spirit Rules #1 and #2: Set Goals and Accomplish Them, and Know the Basics.

I ran up to Mom while everyone was getting ready for practice to tell her what Jacqui's and my plan was. She gave me a big thumbs-up. Yay!

Before we started our usual warm-up and

GIVE ME A
43!

stretches, Jacqui and I had the team gather around so that we were in the middle and everyone else made a circle around us.

"All right, guys, your captains have heard your complaints and now we're responding. We know you want to be more than just the kids who cheer at chess club. Right?"

I tried to meet the eyes of each person while I was talking. That's one of the rules in the book about being a good captain: "Always Make Eye Contact." But I could tell that the team had no idea where I was going with this. Katarina was picking off some nail polish; Tabitha Sue looked at me sweetly, but she also seemed confused. Ian was like, "Uh-huh, so?" Someone wasn't in a good mood today.

"And we also know that you are willing to do whatever it takes to get to the next level," said Jacqui.

A couple more people nodded, but not with the enthusiasm I was hoping for.

"The Grizzlies need to have a goal. Something to work toward besides just getting better. So our goal is going to be to compete at the Washington Get Up and Cheer Competition at the end of the year."

"Yay!" squealed Jared. He leaped up from where he'd been sitting and wrapped his froglike body around one

GIVE ME A 44!

of Matt's beefy arms.

"Dude, get off me!" said Matt, shaking him off like an annoying fly.

Tabitha Sue, the one cheerleader on the team who actually hadn't been complaining lately, looked worried. "You really think we'll be good enough to compete?" she looked like I'd just told her to attempt a heel-stretch while standing on top of a pyramid.

I held up The Spirit Rules book like Rafiki held up Simba to show him off to the rest of the animal kingdom in The Lion King. (side note: I know it's, like, a kids' movie and all, but I still totally heart The Lion King.) "Chill, everyone. I've got a plan."

I told them where the book came from and how it has lots of great cheer secrets about how to make your team stronger, better, more skilled, and most of all, full of spirit. "The Titans have been going by the words in this book for years. Why shouldn't the Grizzlies? We're going to stick to the rules in this book and follow them to a T. But it's not going to be easy."

My mom walked into the circle, nodding in agreement. "You may regret having asked for this, kids. That is,

GIVE ME A 45!

until you're up there on the mat, at a competition of your own, adrenaline pumping through your veins. Believe me, it will be worth it." We all looked at her face, and just seeing the sparkle in my mom's eyes told them that she was speaking from lots of experience.

I'd just gotten a totally brilliant idea!

"Coach Carolyn is right," I said, careful not to call her Mom. "And the Regional Qualifier will be your first glimpse into this world."

"But we won't be competing at the qualifier," Matt blurted out, confused.

"No, we won't," I agreed. "But we _will_ be performing. We're going to have a lot of down time, so we're going to put it to good use and practice our competition mode by performing some cheers and stunts in the practice areas and off to the sides. We'll do some cheers for the Titans, too."

"Let me get this straight," Matt replied in disbelief. "We're going to cheer on the Titans at a cheerleading competition?"

"That's right. We are," I replied.

"Ok," said Ian. "If this spirit book is going to help us, I'm down to see what it's all about."

"Spirit _Rules_, Ian," said Tabitha Sue, coming up to take a closer look at the book. "It's not a ghost story.

GIVE ME A 46!

pay attention."

"Today we're going to work on some of the basics,"
Jacqui said. "Let's master our jumps. I know we've been
working on these for a while, but I want everyone to
get their legs higher than they've ever kicked them
before."

While everyone partnered up to practice one of the
stretching tricks from <u>The Spirit Rules</u>, I told them
a story about a girl from a Southern cali cheer squad
who was one of the best tumblers in her whole region,
but she'd never really perfected her toe touch. Her
team was supposed to be headed to Nationals, but at
Regionals a superharsh judge deducted points for her
sloppy toe touch and being off-count on her jumps. "So
it doesn't matter how good you are at the crazy-hard
stunts. You still have to be awesome at the basic ones,"
I told the squad as I went around correcting postures.
"You don't want to hit a superhard stunt perfectly and
then find out you lost because you were sloppy on a
basic move you could do in your sleep."

After toe touches, I got the team working on
back walkovers, which were pretty shaky for almost
everyone (except Katarina, of course). Ian was
petrified; he practically peed his pants every time
it was his turn to try one. And he kept on insisting

GIVE ME A
47!

on having Matt as his spotter, even though the only spotting Matt's ever done has been in the weight room.

"I don't trust you girls," Ian said, motioning for Matt to come over. "You've got stick arms."

Jacqui and I just looked at each other, knowing this would only lead to both Matt and Ian being sprawled out on the floor.

"We have arms that know exactly how to catch you if you fall," Jacqui said. "If you fall on Matt, you'll probably just crush his wrist. And how will that help the squad?"

It was pretty hilarious to watch this normally macho jock guy so afraid to do a measly back walkover. We spent the rest of practice helping Ian, and we almost didn't realize that Tabitha Sue had gotten hers down perfectly!

"Check it out, guys!" said Jared, flapping his arms excitedly and pointing. "Look at Tabitha Sue!"

Mom, Jacqui, and I all looked over at Tabitha Sue and saw her arch her back until her hands made contact with the ground. Then, to our surprise, her hips went over her head, and she landed one foot at a time.

"I did it again!" she said, beaming. She and Jared gave each other high fives.

"That was crazy good!" I said. I couldn't believe it.

GIVE ME A 48!

Maybe there **WAS** something to these spirit rules.

After practice Mom patted Jacqui and me on the shoulders and told us how great today's practice had been. "Mads, I'm gonna get a few things together. Meet you by the car in fifteen?"

I'm psyched because Jacqui and I are planning on going on another mall run together tomorrow. I'm in **DESPERATE** need of more cheer clothes. The plan is to meet up at our usual spot—the food court (hey, even if it has been only once or

twice, it can be called "the usual"—LOL). I'm also looking forward to it because it will help get my mind off this

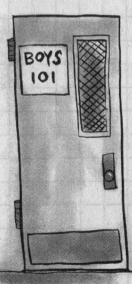

Bevan thing. I can't believe the way he looked when I told him I was busy today. He could totally tell I was lying. I wish I could go "back to the basics" of talking to boys. What if I just tell him how I feel and why I'm avoiding him? Maybe he'll understand. Too bad there isn't a chapter on **THAT** in this Spirit Rules book.

GIVE ME A 49!

## Spirit Rule #3:

Always Prepare for the Unexpected

Most insane day **EVER**!! So, I went to the mall to meet Jacqui and was waiting by Sublicious for her for, like, ten minutes. Finally she texted to say she had the worst headache ever and wasn't coming! So annoying. I still needed to do some shopping for workout clothes—and now I could be on the hunt for cute things to wear to the Regional Qualifier. (Even though we aren't competing, I want to look good for the judges. Who knows? One year it could be me up there, so I want to look my best.) I decided to hit up Score! They always have pretty good sales on sports stuff.

I was looking through some supersoft T-shirts when I felt someone tap me on the shoulder.

"Boo."

I turned around and it was the **LAST** person on earth I'd been hoping to run into. But of course.

GIVE ME A 50!

Because I just can't get a lucky break—it was Bevan.
I mean, it's not that I didn't want to see him . . .
I **LOVE** seeing him. And there he was, looking all
gorgeous and whatnot. It's just the Katie Parker
factor. . . . Grrrr . . .

"Oh, hey. Uh, um," I said, practically stuttering.

He was holding a pair of running
sneakers. How could I have been so
dumb? Going to the biggest sports
store in town and not thinking,
"Hmm, might I possibly run into
Bevan there?" I would have been
better off going to the Yarn Barn
and making my own cheer clothes.

Not a pretty picture.

"Let me guess." He smiled. "You were just on your
way out?"

"Kind of?" I said, knowing I couldn't really get out of
this one so easily.

"Madison, what's up? One minute we were totally cool,
and the next it's like you think I'm an ax murderer or
something. What's going on?"

I tried to think what The Spirit Rules would say
about this situation. Last night I took notes on a
chapter all about communication—and how captains
are supposed to be totally honest with their coaches

GIVE ME A
5!!

and their team—and I knew I couldn't back out again.
I already learned the hard way yesterday that lying
to Bevan felt the opposite of good. So I fessed up.
I told him everything—the whole reason I'd decided
we couldn't actually go on our date as planned, how
Katie had declared Bevan off-limits to every other
cheerleader when the
two of them had broken
up, and how I didn't want
to ruin my chances of
being a Titan by getting together with him and making
Katie angry.

"I really wanted to go on a date with you, but after
you asked me out, it kind of hit me—being seen with
you would be like a death sentence for my chances with
the Titans."

I didn't even realize that I had put down the items
I had been holding at the store as I was talking, and so
had he. And we had just kind of started walking out of
the store together as I continued my "speech."

"And I was too embarrassed to tell you all of that,"
I went on. "So . . . instead, I just avoided you, hoping
you'd just get bored of me. And I wouldn't actually have
to say no to a date with you."

When I was done explaining why I'd been avoiding him,

I finally looked up at his face. I guess I expected him to be angry. But instead his brown eyes looked sort of thoughtful.

"I totally get being so dedicated to a sport that you'd give up anything that gets in the way of being at the top of your game," he said. His face had a look to it that told me that once he made his mind up about something, there was no stopping him from getting what he wanted. "It just sucks that I'm the something that's getting in the way." The corners of his lips curled into a smile as he looked at me. My heart did a little flip.

I was so relieved that I was able to tell him how I've been feeling this whole time. (It also made me feel superembarrassed to tell him that stuff, but at least now I don't have to worry about running away from him anymore.)

"You want to grab something to eat?" he asked. I could hear the hope in his voice. So cute.

I was starving and excited to stretch our talk even longer. So we went to the Wok & Roll for California rolls (my latest obsession). And then we ended up hanging out for, like, hours! We walked all around the mall, not really doing anything but talking.

We tried out those massage chairs in the expensive

GIVE ME A 53!

electronics store and let them go to town on our backs.

"We should really get one of these for the Lounge, don't you think?" I asked.

"Ye-eh-eh-eh-ssss," he stuttered back, mid-vibration.

He leaned back into his chair and wrinkled his brow. I could tell something was the matter.

"You ok?" I asked him. It was strange, because we had just been laughing and joking.

"Yeah, I was just thinking about my buddy Rob. I'd just come from his house before coming here. Actually, he was supposed to come with me to the mall today. But that was before he got hurt."

"Oh." I frowned. "That sucks. He's one of the best players on the team, isn't he?" I asked. "So, what does that mean for the team? Are they gonna replace him?"

Bevan played with the buttons on his chair. "Yeah, probably. And yeah, that does suck, but I'm actually more worried about his actual knee. The doc says he might need major surgery."

Sooo cute! I gave him big points for not being all macho and instead being worried about his friend. Most guys would be freaking out about whether they'd still be able to win as many games. Yet another reason why Bevan

GIVE ME A 54!

was the exact definition of "awesome."

We tried on silly hats at one of the
hat stands, and he took a picture with
his phone of me wearing a Russian-
style hat with fur on the earflaps. I'll
have to ask Katarina if she has one of
those. They're kinda cute!

"Nice. This will be your profile pic
on my phone when you call," he said after he saved the
picture to his phone.

His arm kept brushing against mine when we walked,
and he was like, "Sorry," and I was like, "Sorry," and
then we both laughed.

Sigh. It was soooo much fun. It felt so easy, like
hanging out with a friend (a very, very cute friend).

Unforch, Mom had to pick me up at three 'cuz
she had errands to run after. "Did you have fun with
Jacqui?" she asked when I got into the car.

"Oh. Uh. She didn't show, actually."

"Oh, honey, I would have picked you up," she said,
turning out of the parking lot.

"No, it was cool," I said, flopping my head back
dreamily into the seat. "I hung out with another friend."

"A friend?" Mom looked at me strangely. "Hmm. Ok,"
she said with a little smile.

GIVE ME A
55!

I turned on the radio, and luckily that was the end of the convo. I'm glad she didn't ask me any more questions because I so didn't feel like getting into it with her just then.

Unfortunately, my dreamy feeling didn't last. I went from floating on air to absolutely crazed within one car ride. I didn't mean for this to happen, but now I realized—duh duh duhnnn—I'd hung out with Bevan even though I wasn't supposed to!!!

If Katie finds out, she'll totally go psycho. Even though I'd been trying to avoid hanging out with him before, I'm glad my plan didn't work out. I like him a lot. And it isn't exactly like I hung out with him on purpose. Bumping into someone at the mall isn't the definition of a date. Wait. Another thing—even though it wasn't a "real" date, was this Bevan's and my "first date"? Will he ask me out again? Do I **WANT** him to? He hadn't mentioned a next time. So frustrating!

Later I called Lanie to tell her what happened.

"Madison, what's wrong? You're out of breath."

"I was running. To. Tell. You."

"What? Is everything ok?"

"I just hung out with Bevan Ramsey!" I said, practically all in one breath.

"What? How?"

GIVE ME A 56!

I told her everything that happened this afternoon, and she was so surprised but also excited for me. Go, BFFs!

"Aww, little Madison Hays. All grown up," Lanie joked.

"This is serious!" I said. "What if Katie finds out?"

"Katie won't find out," said Lanie. "Unless Bevan's the kind of guy to brag to the whole soccer team. And even though I'm not the biggest fan of jocks, I actually don't think he's the type to do that."

Phew! That made me feel a little better.

"You promise?" I pleaded.

"Well, obviously I have no control over this. But I do think it's doubtful."

"Sweet! But you know, there is one thing you do have control over . . . ," I hinted.

"What now?"

"Can you just please not tell Evan? He got so weird a few weeks ago when we bumped into Bevan at the mall, and I just don't really want to deal with his attitude right now. I have way too many other things going on."

"Ok, deal. But I'm telling you, I'm not a big fan of secrets. I'm only doing this because I totally heart you."

"Noted!"

☺ Yay!

I hung up the phone and realized I'd missed a call from Jacqui.

GIVE ME A 57!

She didn't even wait for me to say hello when I called back. "Madison, I am so sorry for flaking out today," she said. "I never do that, but I thought this stupid pain would go away with a couple Advil. It just got worse."

"Don't worry about it, Jacqui," I told her. "You'll never believe what happened. But you have to swear not to tell anyone."

"Uh-oh," said Jacqui when I was done telling my story the second time. "Not good news if Katie finds out. But of course your secret's safe with me. I mean, I'll do my very best to keep it. And I'm happy for you. You guys will be such a great couple."

"Whoa! I'm not saying we're gonna be a couple! One date that I'm still not sure counts as a real date doesn't automatically mean boyfriend-girlfriend, right?"

"Well, you know what I mean," said Jacqui. "He seems to like you a lot. He's been following you around like a puppy after practices. Don't act like you haven't noticed!"

"Hee hee—I have." I laughed, thinking about the times he was trying to talk to me about making plans.

"Well, I think you look really cute together," she said.

I didn't say anything, but secretly I absolutely agreed with her.

GIVE ME A 58!

This day sure did not turn out as planned. Instead of keeping my mind off the Bevan thing, I'm way back on it. There's a rule for this in cheer, of course. The book says, "Always Prepare for the Unexpected." You never know what might happen—like, you could have to do a dance to a song you've never even heard before at a competition. Or in Bevan's case, his team lost one of their best players, and now they have to work around it. I should have been thinking about the "Unexpected" rule when I got to the mall earlier this afternoon. Little did I know my whole "avoid Bevan" plan would go entirely off track. Now I just have to hope this doesn't get around the school. If this gets back to Katie, I'll be kissing the Titans good-bye.

GIVE ME A 59!

# Monday, November 22

After practice, outside locker room waitin' for Jacqs

## Spirit Rule #4:
Work Your Team—But Never Push Too Hard

Ummm . . . Whoa. I passed Katie in the halls today, and instead of stopping and saying hey as usual and just talking about whatever, she gave me such a stink eye that I thought maybe, like, her worst enemy was behind me. Then I turned around, and it was just Rose Turnblatt with her too-thick glasses and long hippie skirt, drinking from the water fountain. And as far as I know, Rose and Katie don't have a problem with each other (besides different tastes in fashion). I'm spazzing out. Does she have some kind of freaky "Maddy hung out with Bevan" sixth sense? How in the world would she have found out that Bevan

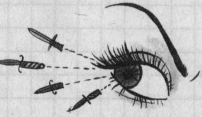

Katie's evil eye:
Lots of mascara, but
still, really evil!!!

GIVE ME A GO!

and I chilled together? Ok, there's another possibility: maybe she decided she doesn't like the uniforms I designed, and every time she looks at me now she's filled with disgust for the uniforms. But no, she would say something if it was about the uniforms, I think. It's so weird because we were so cool with each other recently—ever since I came up with the idea to lend the Titans the Grizzly uniforms at their big game a few weeks ago. Ugh! So confusing. And it's not like I can just go up and talk to her about it. Like, "Hey, Katie. Um. Did you hear Bevan and I went sort of on a date the other day? Oh, you didn't? Ok, never mind!"

Before practice, Mom told Jacqui and me that the Grizzlies have another "game" coming up—we're cheering at the speech club's next competition. It wasn't on our original cheer schedule, but the other day Mom was approached by Principal Gershon, who asked if we could help them out.

Jacqui and I talked about it before the rest of the squad showed up.

"Do you think the team will be cool with cheering at a speech geek competition after what happened last week?" asked Jacqui. She looked a little worried.

"I think so."

But even as I said that, I wasn't so sure. What if

GIVE ME A 6!!

everyone **WOULD** in fact be annoyed about cheering at another loser-ish type of game? So I made sure that practice was especially hard, with new moves to learn, hoping to get everyone into the spirit.

Ian was really upset that he still hadn't gotten his back walkover from the other day, so we started off with those.

"Ian, come here. I'll show you how easy it is," said Tabitha Sue, brushing her hands off on her shirt. She and Katarina had been doing synchronized back walkovers down the length of the mat.

"You? <u>You're</u> gonna show me? I think Katarina probably can do it better."

Tabitha Sue narrowed her eyes. "What's your problem? I can do this just as well as Katarina. Watch." She demonstrated her now **REALLY** good back walkover. She must have been practicing this one at home.

"Point those toes!" Jacqui instructed.

"Oops, sorry!" said Tabitha Sue, coming into her landing.

I don't think Katarina liked being compared to anyone, even if that person was her friend. She did a running start and launched into some backflips while Tabitha Sue, Ian, and Matt all watched in awe.

GIVE ME A
62!

"I am excellent flipper," Katarina declared. I couldn't help laughing, but she was right. That girl can flip.

Katarina and Tabitha Sue worked with Jared and Matt, and Jacqui and I continued spotting Ian. He had finally realized he wasn't going to improve without our help. After a while we got him to arch his back and get his arms to the floor without any spotting. The whole team applauded.

"Look! I did it!" he said from upside down. "Matt! Bro, look!"

"Yeah, I see," said Matt. "But can you get out of it?"

"Uh . . . hold on." Ian scrunched his face—which was getting redder by the second—and tried to lift his legs over his head. But he just couldn't do it. "Ladies? I think I'm stuck."

I helped Ian out of his awkward position. He was panting, and his forehead was beaded with sweat. "Take a breather, Ian. You'll get this. We'll try again tomorrow."

"If I don't get this, I'm quitting. I don't understand how everyone can do this but me," he mumbled angrily, looking at Jared, who had just hit his back walkover. Jacqui whistled and Mom clapped.

"Hey, everyone has their Achilles' heel," I said, patting Ian on the back. He just looked at me blankly.

GIVE ME A 63!

"Their weakness, Ian," I clarified. "Everyone has that one thing that gives them problems. Mine is the scorpion."

Ian started to arch backward without a spotter, trying to get into position again for the back walkover.

"Wait—Ian!" I stopped him before his arms reached the floor. "Come on. You have to relax. If you push yourself too hard on something your body isn't ready for, you might hurt yourself. It's one of the spirit rules."

"It is?"

"Yeah. The rule is actually 'Work Your Team—But Never Push Too Hard.' If I made you get this today, I'd be a bad captain. I even heard last week that a cheerleader at Bay High got put into the hospital because he tried to do a rewind. He hadn't trained to that level yet, but his captain had told him to just 'try' it." I made little quote marks in the air.

"This definitely isn't the football team," he said, shaking his head. "In football, there is no 'try.' You just go for it."

I guess the football captain has different rules for running a team.

At the end of practice we worked on a new cheer for the speech competition that I thought up on the fly:

GIVE ME A 64!

OUR SPEECH TEAM CAN'T BE BEAT.

WE NEVER SAY THE WORD "DEFEAT"!

GO, PORT ANGELES! PORT ANGELES!

GOOOOOO, PORT ANGELES!

It was simple, but our team needed simple so they could feel good about themselves. We added in some basic arm motions, and Jacqui and I did some easy stunts in the front of the line to draw attention. At the end we practiced a thigh stand—it was a little wobbly, but with practice I know it will be great. Mom thought the whole thing looked awesome.

Before everyone left, Mom brought up the car wash we decided to have this weekend. Going to away competitions is not a cheap endeavor, so we'll need to raise some cashola to cut down on the costs. But if what Lanie was saying the other day is true, I'm pretty sure the Titans aren't sweating over it. I guess that's just the way it works. Anyway, what better way for people to give thanks on Thanksgiving than to help spread school spirit by sending the Grizzlies to the qualifier?

"Hope you're all ready to roll up your sleeves on Saturday," said Mom.

"Aren't car washes, like, a chick thing?" asked Matt. His arms were crossed over his chest defensively.

GIVE ME A 65!

"Excuse me?" said Jacqui. "I smell some sit-ups coming on," she warned.

"Yeah, Matt, get over yourself," said Tabitha Sue, rolling her eyes. "You know you love any excuse to take your shirt off."

"Ahem," said Mom. "This will be a shirts-on type of car wash. That means you, too, Ian."

"Hey," said Jared, "why can't us guys work on our tans? Right, fellas?" Jared jabbed his elbow into Matt.

"I changed my mind," said Ian with a look of horror on his face. I guess he must have agreed with the rest of the team that the image of Jared shirtless would probably drive away any possible customers. "I'm down for shirts on," he said, and smiled angelically.

"All right, guys, don't be late."

I looked for Bevan right after practice but couldn't find him in the gym. I haven't seen him all day and it's so weird. Of course when I was avoiding him, he was everywhere. Now when I want to see him, he's hard to find! I didn't want to push my luck and end up face-to-face with Katie and her evil eye, so I didn't stay in the gym for long. I stuck my head into the weight room and just kind of hung outside the boys' locker room for a few, pretending to check my messages.

GIVE ME A 66!

Jacqui spotted me. "You waiting for someone?"

"Oh, uh . . ." I was gonna deny it, but then I realized, who cares? Jacqui's my friend. And she already said she likes the idea of the two of us together.

"You know. B." I leaned against the smooth, cool walls, tracing my fingers in the cracks between the tiles.

"I think I saw the guys peace out of practice early." she frowned.

"Oh. Ok, thanks for letting me know. I would have stood here like a nerd for, like, who knows how long?"

"Eventually you would have figured it out," she said, smiling.

"Right."

We decided to walk over to Steak & Fries and grab a bite before going home. It's just what I need after this weird day with the whole Katie thing. I guess maybe I should take some of my own advice to Ian and just chill, not push it too far . . . right?

GIVE ME A 67!

## Spirit Rule #5:
It Takes a Team to Build a Pyramid

Soooooooo. I've got a problem. Not a GINORMOUS problem, but still, it's kind of big. I'm hanging in the Lounge, reading through The Spirit Rules and taking some notes in my journal, when Clementine and Hilary come up to me! I could tell from the looks on their faces that this wasn't a "Hey, how's it goin'?" kind of visit. Which made me panic: Were they gonna say something about Bevan and me? It would be so like them to do Katie's dirty work.

But what they had to say took me completely by surprise.

"So, your friend with the blue hair has been talking to our teammates, you know," said Hilary. She was chewing her gum with so much force that I was worried her jaw would dislocate. Then I realized that would mean she'd have to stop talking for a while, and I

GIVE ME A
68!

thought, "Cool—that wouldn't be so bad!"

I had hoped this thing with Lanie and her article wasn't gonna come back to haunt me. Wishful thinking 🙁. Thing is, a part of me IS relieved they didn't say anything about Bevan.

"Yeah, she's interviewing them for an article for the Daily Angeles." I forced my face to look blank, like I didn't really know what they could possibly be worried about. Yeah, me—Little Miss Innocent.

Hilary took out a compact mirror and started applying a lip gloss with a label that read "The Big Glossip." All the Titan cheerleaders have been wearing it lately— apparently it stings their lips but it makes 'em look

before... after!

The Big Glossip

like Angelina Jolie's. Typical cheerleader mentality. No pain, no gain.

Clementine decided to step in, since Hilary was "busy."

"Yeah, we know about the article," Clementine said with a wave of her hand. Like she was trying to show that anything I had to say was unimportant. "But she's asking all kinds of shady questions about, like,

GIVE ME A 69!

funding and stuff. The team is worried she's going to say bad things about us. It sounds to us like your friend might be trying to ruin our reputation."

## PSSST! It's A SECRET!

I guess I didn't realize how bad Lanie's questions would sound. But apparently they sound so bad that they're spooking the entire Titan squad. And could that mean that maybe they have something to hide?!?

"Lanie?" I said with as much surprise in my voice as I could muster. "She so wouldn't do that." That is the truth. She wouldn't make the Titans look bad ON PURPOSE. If she finds something that's unfair about how they are getting money for all their trips and uniforms and things like that, well, that's another story. "But you know," I continued, "it's her job to ask questions. She's a journalist. But maybe just tell the girls on the team not to answer questions they don't feel comfortable with."

"Ha!" Clementine huffed. "As if it were that easy." She tilted her head toward Hilary and gave her a look. "Because <u>some</u> girls on the team don't know when to

GIVE ME A 70!

keep their mouths shut. Anyway, aren't you and Lanie, like, twins separated at birth or something?" she said, rolling her eyes.

"She is my best friend, if that's what you mean."

Just then Clementine got all up in my face and was like, "Listen, the Titans do <u>not</u> need bad publicity before Regionals. And the team is stressing out big-time from all these questions. Rein her in, Madison. Katie and I are depending on you. Or else."

At the mention of Katie's name, I felt a little nauseous.

"Hey, what about me?" asked Hilary, suddenly interested in the convo.

"Just follow me," said Clementine, shaking her head, apparently totally annoyed.

So, great. What to do now? Katie's all peeved about Lanie's article and probably something else, too, which I'm trying to figure out (Bevan? The uniforms? Something I can't even guess at?). Now the Triumvirate wants me to talk to my BEST FRIEND and ask her to stop doing her JOB as a journalist? And if I don't? What? The Titans will be mad at me? Why do I always feel like I'm one false move away from not realizing my dream? It's like trying to do a pyramid with one person. SERIOUSLY?? The Spirit Rules

GIVE ME A 7!!

has another rule: "It Takes a Team to Build a Pyramid." which I think also means that one person can't take on the weight of everything. I feel like so much is just coming down on little ol' me. And it's kind of insane! THIS pyramid? Is about to topple.

I really need to talk to someone. Too bad I can't ask Lanie for help with the Titans having a problem with her article since the problem is, well, Lanie.

## AFTER PRACTICE, LOCKER ROOM

At practice we decided to take the team on a run. You can't be a good cheerleader without endurance! And today was actually pretty warm for November in Washington, which meant that we were all sweating ten minutes into it. Jacqui and I kept the pace up for the rest of the team and made sure to run ahead of them to set a good example. I took that chance to be alone with her to ask for advice about the Lanie problem.

"You should talk to her," Jacqui suggested, after I'd told her what happened earlier with Clementine and Hilary. "Believe me, I know what happens when you make those girls mad."

"Ugh, but wouldn't that mean giving in to their silliness?" I said, breathless from talking while running.

GIVE ME A
72!

Jacqui shook her head. "No. It would mean making life easier on you."

"Ok, Jacqui. But it's not exactly easy to tell your best friend not to write what she needs to write." I looked behind me to make sure the rest of the team wasn't lagging behind.

"I think if you explain the situation the right way, she'll understand that this article is putting you in a bad position. She's your best friend—don't you think she'll understand?"

"I guess," I said, but I wasn't sure. Even though she's my bestie, when it comes to her writing, she can be pretty serious about it.

We came to a steep hill and agreed on no more talking.

I just hope the talk I have with Lanie won't be as tough as that run.

# wednesday, November 24

Lunchtime, school Caf

## Spirit Rule #6:

The Team Always Comes First

So, today is already turning out to be one of those days. I mean, some good stuff has happened—ok, so it's mostly bad, but if I don't write down the good stuff, I might go insane!!! This whole week has been just too much to handle. T.G. tomorrow is Thanksgiving—I totally need a break from all the D-R-A-M-A!

First the good: It's my favorite lunch today—baked ziti. I got a huge serving from the lunch lady who likes me the best and settled in between Lanes and Evan. We sat at our table and caught up on each other's lives. I'm soooo happy that I got to hang out with Lanie and Evan (even though Lanie's article is still on my mind).

And I've been feeling like I haven't spoken to Evan in years, so it was nice that we got to be just the three of us. Like old times ☺.

well, it **WAS** fun, until halfway through lunch. We

GIVE ME A 74!

were laughing and joking around, having a blast for a while, and then Lanie asked a simple question.

"So, Evan," said Lanie, eating a tofu stir-fry she brought from home, "when's the next SuperBoy coming out? Do you have plans for another soon?"

"Yeah, E, come on—the masses want more!" I pleaded jokingly.

And that's where things went downhill.

The bad: Evan's mood totally changed as soon as Lanie and I asked him about SuperBoy. He barely looked up from his Chicken McNuggets when she asked. (He actually smuggles his fave lunch into the caf every few weeks, after he meets up with the delivery guy from McDonald's on the front steps. It's a miracle he hasn't gotten caught yet.)

"Yeah." He shrugged. "I'm working on it."

"So?" I gave Lanie a what's-with-him look. "Tell us what it's about."

"Top secret," he said, mixing hot sauce with BBQ sauce. "You'll see it when you see it."

"All right—we'll be holding our breath," said Lanie, laughing.

Evan acting like that made my blood boil! All of a sudden he's becoming Mr. Mysterious on us? This is Evan. The guy I've known since I was five. And

GIVE ME A 75!

now he wants to pretend like he has something up his sleeve? So annoying. Of course, I find him even more interesting when he backs away like this. Which is just sooo me.

Lanie changed the subject. "So, who watched last night's episode of <u>Top Chef</u>?" she asked. The three of us L-O-V-E this show—which I always think is funny since Lanie is really anti-television. Except for the History channel.

I was relieved that she didn't bring up cheerleading, but the situation was whirling around in my head all through our lunch. I know I'll have to bring up my convo with Clementine and Hilary sooner or later, before Lanie asks something that will make the Titans really mad at me. And the more I think about it, the more I realize that Lanie HAS been hanging around the Titans more and more this week, and showing up at their practices. How did I not notice that before Clem and Hilary talked to me about it? I decided that I would just tell Lanie

GIVE ME A 76!

about the Titans' bugging out and see if that might get her to change her questions a bit. Maybe get her to be more on the DL. Ugh—I'm dreading this convo. Who am I to tell Lanie how to do her job? That's like Lanie telling me how to do a layout.

"Madison?" asked Lanie. "Earth to Madison."

Evan waved a handful of fries in front of me.

"Oh, sorry," I said, my face red with embarrassment. Like I was worried she could read my thoughts. "Just daydreaming . . ."

"Ohhhkaaay," said Lanie, looking at Evan and making the "crazy person" sign with her finger.

But I wimped out on saying anything to her just then. It wouldn't have been a good idea to have our talk in front of moody Evan, anyway. And I just wanted to try to enjoy the three of us being together. Even though Evan's 'tude about his SuperBoy wasn't exactly enjoyable. I'll talk to her about it later. I promise.

## AFTER PRACTICE, PARKING LOT

I waited until right before practice. I did a quick scan of the room before my eyes landed on her in the middle of a crowd of stretching Titans. She was easy to find. She was in fancy reporter mode with her clipboard, notepad, and tape recorder and was

GIVE ME A 7?!

holding one of the younger cheerleaders hostage. The
cheerleader was shaking her head—probably denying
some pressing journalistic question. Then I saw Katie
across the room. She had just spotted me, too, and she
gave me a little nod as if to say, "You heard what Clem
said. Go talk to her."

I went up to Lanie as soon as her interviewee walked
away. My heart was beating superfast. I was really
torn. On the one hand, I didn't want my best friend to
think I doubted her, and on the other, I didn't want to
make Katie hate me any more than she already did and
ruin my chances of ever becoming a Titan.

"So . . . I kind of have to talk to you about
something."

"What?" Lanie asked, but her attention was
definitely focused on the Titans. The flyers were
practicing their full-up cupies with their partners.
Lanie wrote something down on her notepad.

"I don't really know how to say this to you."
That seemed to get her attention for sure. She put
her pen into her pocket. "Oh, sorry," she said. "What?
Do I have, like, toilet paper hanging out of my pants?"
She laughed, turning to check her backside.

"No, no, you look fine. You look really cute, actually,"
I said, pointing to her secretary-style shirt and

GIVE ME A
78!

high-waisted vintage skirt. "It's about the article."
She could probably tell at this point, by looking at my
face, that I wasn't going to be saying anything helpful.

"Ok. Spit it."

"The Titans are worried you're going to say
something bad about them, even though I know you
won't. You know—they can't be getting bad press right
now, with all these competitions coming up. And some of
the girls are getting, like, psyched out by some of the
interview questions," I said, rolling my eyes.

"So you're saying . . . ?"

"They asked me to talk to you about toning it down
a bit. And also to make sure you don't make them look
bad in the article." I could tell as I said it that it was
already going somewhere very bad. And I had purposely
decided not to tell her why I was saying anything at all
in the first place—that Clem had suggested I should
talk to Lanie "or else." I didn't want her to think that I
was asking her to kill her dream so that in the future
I could maybe have mine.

"Tone it down?" she huffed. "I can't 'tone down'
reporting. Besides, the Titans are supposed to be, like,
the best team at Port Angeles. If they have nothing to
hide, then why are they so worried?"

"I know!" I agreed. "They're totally acting weird. But

GIVE ME A
79!

I promised Clementine and all them that I'd talk to you about it."

"Oh," she said coldly.

That was SO not how I'd planned this talk to go.

Then she turned around and took a few steps back. "You know, I thought you'd be hyped that I'm doing an article about cheerleading. This is what I get for trying to take more of an interest in my best friend's sport, huh? But I see how it is—you're choosing the Titans over your best friend. Nice, Mads." Lanie rolled her eyes with disgust and started to walk away.

"No, Lanes, it's not like that—"

"Well, it sounds like it is. It sounds like you don't trust me, and you would rather protect them than me."

I didn't even know what to say. She was sort of right. In a way, I HAD chosen them over her. Some friend I am.

"You know what," continued Lanie, "since I have nothing to hide or be secretive about, I'll show you the article before it goes to print and you can see for yourself if it meets your so-called friends' standards." And then she walked away from me.

I stood there for a while, stunned by what had just happened. We've never had a fight like this before. Like, in the past, we may have disagreed about what movies

GIVE ME AN 80!

to see or where to hang out on the weekend—stupid stuff. Our worst fight had been when we were ten and I was upset because she was hanging out with Evan more than me. But this was kinda serious. And I didn't even really have time to digest it because I had to go start practice.

Today we had the squad do a ton of pikes and toe touches, concentrating on good form. But Jacqui and Mom were pretty much doing most of the work because my head was completely on another planet. I kept hearing Lanie's words in my head all through practice and couldn't concentrate. I was a total joke.

"Jared, we said point, not flex!" said Jacqui.

"Sorry! Sorry!" said Jared. He shook his head, obviously annoyed at himself. "It's like, I say in my head to point, and then when I'm up in the air, I just forget to do it!"

Tabitha Sue nodded, agreeing. "I keep forgetting to keep my wrists straight."

"All right," said Mom. "Let's divide and conquer. Half the team goes with Jacqui, the other half with Madison. I want you each to take turns working individually with your captain and have her watch you. No one is leaving without three perfect jumps in a row."

The whole squad started practicing, but when Matt

GIVE ME AN 8!!

did his pike in front of me, I was so far off in la-la land, I didn't see that his arms were totally wobbly instead of straight.

"Madison!" my mom yelled. "Did you not just see Matt's wrists?"

Matt groaned.

"Oh, uh . . . yeah, sorry. I missed it."

"Do it again, Matt," Mom instructed.

It kind of went on like this for a while. I kept on missing things, and Mom finally came up to me.

"Honey, I don't know what's wrong with you, but you need to come back to the team. Whatever it is, you'll have to deal with it after practice. And I'll be happy to talk to you about it. Ok?"

She totally had a point. Spirit Rule #6: "The Team Always Comes First." I had to put my head back in the game, as they say, and think about the Lanie thing not on practice time.

As soon as everyone left to go to the locker rooms, Clementine, Hilary, and Katie came up to me to ask what happened when I spoke to Lanie.

"She promised she'd show the article to me first to see if it's ok," I told them.

Clementine looked as happy as Clementine could look. "Good." She smiled. "So that's taken care of." She looked

GIVE ME AN 82!

at Katie, who was looking at me like I just ran over her dog. "Are we good, Katie?" she asked.

Hilary turned to Katie too as they waited for her next set of orders.

"Yeah, it's cool. For now."

Hilary looked at me and shrugged. It was like she was saying, "I have no idea what's up her butt." Which was actually pretty funny because I didn't really know that Hilary had any thoughts of her own. And also, it was probably one of the only times Hilary and I would ever agree on something. But I wish I knew what was going on in Katie's head.

Ok, another good thing happened today ☺. I was walking toward the parking lot when I heard someone call my name.

"Madison!"

I turned around, knowing that the only face that adorable voice could belong to was his. Sigh. Happiness.

"Oh. Hi!" I didn't mean to sound so excited. But it had been a while. (Ok, so it had been, like, a day.)

"I saw you and the Titans having a serious-looking talk when I passed by the gym. Everything ok?" he asked.

GIVE ME AN 83!

I could smell bubble gum on his lips, and he did this cute thing where he stopped his gum chewing and raised his eyebrows until I answered him. Like he was waiting for my next move or something.

"Oh, just some more cheer drama." I rolled my eyes in the direction of the gym.

He smiled. "Those Titans giving you a hard time about us?"

I almost fainted when he said the word "us," because I was not expecting that at all. I felt my face get all red. We are an "us"? Woohoo!!!

"Us?" I squeaked. "Like, you and me?"

"I was joking," he said quickly. "I just mean, are they upset because we hung out the other day?"

"Oh! Right!" I smacked myself on the forehead like a complete dork. But he did say "us." I didn't, like, imagine it. So . . . does that mean he thinks there is an "us" but is too embarrassed to admit he's thinking that? Or did he really just mean "us," like, in the one-day sense of the word, like "us, that day in the mall and only that day," in which case I'm totally humiliated. Like, beyond.

"Yeah, I don't know if they know about it," I said quickly, hoping this awkwardness would disappear immediately. "I didn't really tell anyone about us hanging out except for, like, Lanie. Um, did you?" Yikes. That

GIVE ME AN 84!

was a lie. I told Jacqui, too. But it's not like she's gonna run and tell anyone.

"No." He shook his head. "I just figured—cheerleaders, drama. What you told me the other day about Katie making me 'off-limits.'" He laughed.

"Oh, no," I said, shaking my head. "It's actually something else entirely. Some article Lanie's writing for the Daily." I was glad that I didn't have to make this up. I'm the worst liar EVER!

I was also glad we had moved our chat away from the "us" portion of the convo. He must think I'm one of those girls who always wants a boyfriend. Great. We talked a little more, but when we said good-bye he was just like, "'K, talk to you later, Maddy." And it's cute that he calls me "Maddy" instead of "Madison," but still, WHEN will he talk to me later, exactly? What does that mean? Will he call me? Text me? Are we gonna hang out again?

WHAT IS WRONG WITH BOYS????!!!!

## EVENING, MY CRIB

Back home when we sat down to dinner, Mom wanted to know why I was in such a weird mood earlier at practice. And, like, totally out of the blue, she asked, "Hey, I noticed Lanie's been hanging a lot around the

GIVE ME AN 85!

Titans. What's going on with that?" So I decided to tell her everything. It felt good to chat with Mom about friend stuff, like we used to. It's been a while.

Mom told me that when she was just trying out for the team as a cheerleader, two of her closest friends also tried out. When they didn't make it, they decided they hated the Titans for it. So of course it was always way AWK every time my mom just wanted to be, like, chilling with her cheer friends, because the friends who didn't make the team would give her all sorts of attitude.

"And one day, Marge and Tiffany got really upset with me. They'd noticed I was forgetting important things we'd always done together, like our annual Halloween sleepover. At first I told them, 'Cheer is everything to me.' But you know what?" she asked, shaking her head and looking into the distance.

"What?" I asked. "That sounds about right. Doesn't the team always come first?"

"Sure, the team does always come first." Mom smiled.

I felt like I was missing something. If I was right, why was she smirking like that?

"The question is, <u>which</u> team comes first?" she continued.

GIVE ME AN 86!

There it was!

"Cheer is important—don't get me wrong. But you have a life, too. You don't want to lose your friends. Sometimes the team that has to come first is your friends or your family. You know Lanie—she would never do anything to hurt you, including writing an article that would ruin your chances of becoming a Titan. And even if that article revealed some things about the Titans that aren't so great, you should support her right to write the truth. She always supports you."

I realized I hadn't even touched my vegetable couscous.

"I should have stood up to them, right, Mom?"

"I can't tell you what you should or shouldn't have done," Mom said. "But Team Titans will one day be a thing of the past. Your friendship with Lanie—that's a team that'll last forever."

I couldn't believe how wrong I'd been. And hearing Miss Everything Cheer saying that cheer didn't always come first? That was REALLLLLLYYYY huge.

I ran upstairs to see if Lanie was online. She wasn't, so I called her. The phone rang and rang. No answer. She was totally avoiding my calls! Urgh!

"Evan," I said over v-chat, "please tell Lanie I have to talk to her and that it is a matter of life or death."

GIVE ME AN
87!

"Um, I really don't want to get in the mid—"

I cut him off. "Evan, I need you. She won't listen to me," I pleaded.

He fiddled with his mouse and typed something—probably chatting with someone else.

"Hello?"

"I'm thinking about it," said Evan. "All right, fine. Just this once. But if she says no, then that's it. I'm not begging her for your friendship."

"All right," I said. We x-ed out of v-chat. Then I waited. Finally Lanie rang me on-screen.

"Lanes, I am so, so, so sorry for what I said today. It was totally wrong. I should have always trusted you and not even thought about listening to Clementine and all of them. I know you'll do an awesome job reporting. And whatever you need to say, well, that's your job and it is up to you."

Lanie just sat there looking at the screen for a while. Finally she spoke. "And?"

"And . . ." I wasn't sure what else to say. I thought I had said it all. But then it came to me: "I will never choose the team over you again. You're my best friend. Aaaand . . . I was really wrong. I was worried the Titans would use this against me and never take me on their team."

Lanie's face softened. "Thanks, Mads. But now I'm

GIVE ME AN
88!

kinda sorry . . . I didn't think about what an awkward position this put you in, knowing how badly you want to be on their team. I'M sorry. That was really careless of me. So . . . they threatened you?"

"Eh, doesn't really matter. So, can we call it even?" I asked hopefully.

"All righty," Lanie said, nodding her head. "That works. But don't _ever_ do that again!" She smiled. "Just trust me, ok?"

"I know—I will. And I'll stand up to the Titans if they talk to me about you again."

"Nah, don't worry about it. I'll make your life easier and just do some behind-the-scenes reporting from now on. I've gotten most of what I needed from the interviews by now anyway."

"Oh, well, good, I guess," I said. I felt guilty because I didn't want her article not to be good because of me. "But really, if you still need to—"

"It's cool," said Lanie. "Besides, fear isn't a good look for you. I wouldn't want you walking around wondering what they're gonna say to you next."

And THAT is why she's my bestie ☺.

I'm so glad that we made up. Hurrah!!! I don't know what I'd do without Lanes, even for a few days. Phew, that was close.

GIVE ME AN 89!

# Saturday, November 27

Evening, Sofa City

# Spirit Rule #7:

## Don't Just Go Through the Motions

I can't believe I'm finally vegging out—I'm sooo exhausted. On the upside, we made a ton of cash at the car wash fund-raiser. It was a gorgeous day, so everyone in town came to the school parking lot to give their cars a good cleaning, even though it was a holiday weekend. As a surprise for the team, Mom gave us T-shirts to wear that read "Get Scrubbed by a Grizzly!"

"Aw, Mom! These are adorable!"

Mom smiled, her hands on her hips. "It was easy," she said. "And I figure you'll be able to use these for future car washes too."

Our first customer drove up. Two college-age girls driving a blue BMW rolled down the windows.

"Hello, ladies," said Ian, pushing up his T-shirt sleeves to show off more of his biceps.

"What are you raising money for?" asked the

GIVE ME A 90!

girl with long, curly hair.

"Uh. Um. It's for my . . . my . . ." Ian was having trouble finishing the sentence.

Tabitha Sue stepped in, happy to have found an opportunity to embarrass Ian. "It's for his cheerleading team. Our cheerleading team. We're the Grizzlies," she said, pointing to her T-shirt. Ian turned bright red.

The curly-haired girl looked at her friend, giggled, and pointed to Ian. "If we get our car washed, will you throw in a cheer for free?"

By now, everyone was curious as to what had made Ian lose his cool.

"Of course he'll do it!" said Jacqui, patting him on the back. "Right?"

Ian, Tabitha Sue, and I got to work on the car, and Ian mumbled the whole time about what was waiting for him when he was done cleaning the BMW. "Maybe they'll forget," Ian said to me.

"Oh, I really doubt it."

When it was time for the girls to pay, Ian held out his hand to take their money, but they refused. "Cheer first, pay after."

Ian halfheartedly did some hand motions as he cheered:

LET'S GET FIRED UP!

GET ROUGH, GET TOUGH, GET MEAN!

GIVE ME A 9!!

LET'S GET FIRED UP

AND ROLL RIGHT OVER THAT TEAM!

The girls hooted and clapped when he was finished.

"Very impressive," said the other girl in the car.

"Really?" asked Ian.

"Yeah. You were great. And very cute. Here." She handed him a ten-dollar tip.

He was still staring at the tip when they waved good-bye. We all started cracking up.

"That was awesome!" said Matt. "Cheerleading gets older chicks!"

"I guess so!" agreed Ian.

"Actually," I said, "cheerleading is all about putting on a show to please the audience. You have to look excited and happy when you're onstage. That's why you see a lot of cheerleaders making funny, crazy faces when they're stunting. They know they have to be in performer mode."

"Your point is . . . ?" asked Matt.

"Ian put on a show for our customers just now, and look where it got us!" I pointed to the ten-dollar tip Ian had just placed in our fund-raising pile. "A big tip. It's up there in the rules. Spirit Rule #7: 'Don't Just Go Through the Motions.' A team at last year's Nationals scored the lowest points of anyone because the judges

GIVE ME A 92!

said they looked like they weren't having fun."

"Ouch—that sucks," said Ian.

"Huh," said Matt. "Interesting."

So from that point on, every time there was a group of girls in a car, Ian and Matt volunteered to cheer for them. And they smiled through the whole thing. Each time, they'd get the largest tips. I would have thought it was unfair—had the money not been going toward our own team.

And in between washes we all practiced our back walkovers, and Ian actually got his—without a spotter! I guess having girls to impress made him more confident.

Now we won't have to cough up as much money per person for the trip, which is UH—MAZING. More for me to spend on materials for this totally fab dress I'm designing. . . .

As it turns out, the Titans barely had to do anything to pay for their trip or the cost of competing at the qualifier. (Just as I thought.) According to Lanie, their idea of fund-raising is asking their parents to swipe a credit card. It's funny, cuz it never really bothered me before. But now that we Grizzlies actually had to raise money for our trip, the difference is even more obvious. So unfair sometimes! Hmm . . . maybe Lanie's onto something. . . .

GIVE ME A
93!

# Monday, November 29

Time to pass out, bedfordshire

## Spirit Rule 8:

Find moments for your team to shine

*Compare & Contrast*

Yay! Gooo, Grizzlies! We did pretty well at the speech competition overall. Jacqui, Mom, and I were superproud of the team. It was only a teensy bit awkward at first because the speech geeks weren't used to having anyone besides themselves talk at their competitions (um, yeah, so there were a few dirty looks from the peanut gallery).

When we first walked into the room, I was thinking there was no way we'd be able to get this crowd hyped up. Everyone, from the students to the judges, was wearing what looked like a business suit. We Grizzlies definitely

GIVE ME A 94!

Speech geek attire

stood out from the crowd! I'd heard that these speech competitions were serious, but I'd never seen one in person. I was like, "Oh, man—this is gonna be rough."

We stood at the front of the room facing the slightly amused stares of everyone in the audience. Tabitha Sue gave me a nervous smile, so I made sure to look extra confident. I knew she was worried about being a stunt base for the first time in front of an audience.

"Let's open with the new cheer," Jacqui instructed.

OUR SPEECH TEAM CAN'T BE BEAT. WE NEVER SAY THE WORD DEFEAT! GO, PORT ANGELES! GO, PORT ANGELES! GOOOOO, PORT ANGELES!

Matt did a low V while everyone else was doing a high V, but that was really the worst of it. We ended the cheer (the "GOOOOO, PORT ANGELES!" part) with a flawless thigh stand. Katarina was the flyer and Tabitha Sue was one of the bases. She did great! But I was glad we had run through these motions a lot during practice.

VS.

cheerleader attire

GIVE ME A 95!

The first person to give his speech looked really scared as he approached the front of the room. After a couple of seconds I realized I recognized him from my gym class the year before. He was the kid who always showed up late and hated to wear the shorts that were part of our dress code. Instead, he'd show up in the kind of jeans that looked like he wore them when he was ten. Like, all badly fitted and too short. Then he'd get docked from class. He was always so quiet—I couldn't imagine him willing to make a speech in front of multiple people. His teammates looked like they were getting really worried that he was going to wuss out. I know I would be pretty upset if he was on my squad.

His hands were locked at his sides while he mumbled his opening lines under his breath. It was so bad that most people were craning their necks to hear him better. I think he either said something about "constitutional haste" or "pharmaceutical waste," but who could tell? And then he did the worst possible thing for someone with stage fright: He looked straight at the audience. It was like he suddenly realized everyone was watching him. His mouth opened, then closed, then opened again.

He reminded me of Lanie's pet fish, Spike. When we

GIVE ME A 96!

were little, she'd tried to convince Evan and me that his little mouth movements were really his way of talking to us. "See?" Lanie used to say. "One open mouth and closed mouth move means 'Hello,' and open close open means 'How are you?' I taught him that." She'd smiled proudly. I'd believed her until Evan started telling Lanie that he swore Spike had mouthed that he wanted Evan to take him out of the tank so he could watch TV with us. Lanie had insisted that she hadn't taught him how to mouth that and that if Evan took him out he'd die. "Not if you teach him how to mouth 'I need water,'" Evan had joked.

"Chester?" asked the teacher adviser.

I snapped back to the present.

"Chester, you'll need to speak up or you'll have to step down, I'm afraid."

I couldn't stand to watch Chester struggle.

"Come on, guys, let's do something really quick to pump him up," I whispered to my team. Spirit Rule #8 says that sometimes you have to look for just the right moment during a game to do something unexpected. Something that will make your team stand out. From one look at my team, I could see that the Grizzlies were finding it just as painful as I was to sit and watch this kid drown in his own embarrassment.

GIVE ME A
97!

"What's the plan?" asked Jacqui.

"The 'Pride' cheer," I suggested. This was something we've been practicing lately. It wasn't our most flawless cheer, but Jared, Matt, Ian, Tabitha Sue, and Katarina all nodded in agreement, so I knew that the team was at least ready to try it out. We stood up and did our quick cheer:

PRIDE (CLAP)

SPIRIT (CLAP)

COME ON, CROWD, LET'S HEAR IT!

STAND UP AND SCREAM,

PORT ANGELES SPEECH TEAM!

Jacqui launched herself into an awesome banana jump, fully arching her body into the air and extending her arms and legs. That was good thinking on her feet, since we hadn't planned on that move being part of the cheer. A few people clapped, and one person in the room said, "whoa," which I think was major props for us, considering the crowd. And the best part was, that Chester kid seemed to get his act together after we'd taken the attention from him for a bit. So when it was his turn to speak again, he cleared his throat, slicked his hair back, and started his speech from the beginning. And rocked it! Quick thinking, Mads (pat on the back for me)!

GIVE ME A 98!

After the competition (which our school won, BTW—hey, hey!), Mom handed everyone permission forms to bring home to parents for the Regional Qualifier trip.

"Don't forget to get a signature from your parent," Mom said as each squad member took a form on our way back to the locker rooms.

"Hey, Mom, can I go?" I joked.

"Yeah, I'll consider it," she said sarcastically.

Jacqui and I started walking to the locker room together. We let the rest of the team file past us toward the gym so we would have a few moments to talk, captain to captain.

"I think the Spirit Rules book is paying off, huh?" she asked. We were standing by one of the science labs.

"I feel bad saying it, but I am kinda surprised at how great we're shaping up," I said. I leaned one hand behind me against a locker to stretch my wrist.

"Did you see Tabitha Sue and that thigh stand? She hit every mark perfectly," said Jacqui, looking back toward the room where the speech competition was clearing out.

"I know!" I said, switching hands. "It was pretty incredible."

"The whole team really is working hard these days,"

GIVE ME A
99!

Jacqui pointed out. "I think we should get everyone on the team to really nail their back walkovers, plus one more new move, and then show them off at the Regional Qualifier when everyone else is practicing. That way, the Grizzlies can feel like they're bringing something to the table too."

"And if they can stand the heat of the big competitions, then I think we'd really stand a chance at one of our own," I said, thinking of the novice competition at the end of the year.

"Totes," Jacqui agreed, high-fiving me.

I hadn't planned on talking about the Bevan and Katie thing with her, but it just felt like the right moment. Jacqui's one of the few people who really understand where I'm coming from, since she's experienced Katie's strange rules firsthand.

"Can I tell you something and you promise not to say 'I told you so'?" I asked her. She looked at me suspiciously at first, which by now I know is just Jacqui's way of figuring out the situation.

"No, I can't promise. But I'll try." She smiled.

"I know you warned me about liking Bevan, but you also said you thought we're cute together."

Jacqui just smiled again. "Ok, good," I thought. So she wouldn't be annoyed that I was bugging her about

GIVE ME A 100!

Bevan. We continued on into the locker room. I told her how much I like Bevan—like, seriously like him—and how we've been flirting a lot lately. I also admitted to her that I was secretly upset that he hadn't asked me out again after we'd hung out at the mall that time. Actually, now that I'm thinking about it, I haven't heard anything from him in a couple of days. Of course, I could like, text him or something. But I don't want him to think I'm super into him or anything.

I hate thinking about this stuff.

I told Jacqui how Katie's been acting really nasty to me ever since the "mall date" but that I couldn't be sure if the reason was because she'd found out Bevan and I had gone out, or something else entirely.

"Mads! I warned you this might happen!" said Jacqui, fumbling with her locker combo.

"Precisely why I asked you not to say 'I told you so'!" I whispered. "And let's keep it down, please. I don't need the whole team to know my business." I could tell that Katarina and Tabitha Sue were looking over in our direction. "So . . . do you think she knows?" I asked her.

"Katie's superpopular, so anything she does—and anything someone she's dating or <u>used</u> to date is doing—is, like, instant gossip," said Jacqui, folding up her gym towel. "I wouldn't be surprised if someone saw

GIVE ME A
101!

you and Bevan and ran to tell her about it."

"Ohmigod, you think?" I asked. It was scary but kind of flattering at the same time. Probably the one and only time in my whole life that something I did would be interesting enough to whisper about in the hallways. Madison Hays, Gossip Starter.

Jacqui shrugged. "Yeah. So I'd say she knows."

"I was afraid of that," I said gloomily. I zipped my cheer clothes into my bag and collapsed on the bench, suddenly feeling totally overwhelmed.

Tabitha Sue came over looking concerned. "You ok?" she asked.

"Oh, yeah. Just really tired, I guess." As a captain, I didn't want my team to know I was down. As they say in the Spirit Rules book, "Smile through the pain."

"So what are you gonna do?" Jacqui asked me, once Tabitha Sue went into the bathrooms.

"I have no idea," I said. "I was so distant with Bevan at first. I'd done a really good job of avoiding him, you know? That ended right after the mall date. Now I

GIVE ME A 102!

can't stop thinking about him." We closed our lockers and waved good-bye to the rest of the team.

"Make your rest!" said Katarina, doing her best to tell us to get a good night's sleep.

Jacqs and I both tried not to laugh at our friend.

"Maybe you should just follow your heart," said Jacqui philosophically. "And stop caring so much about what the Titans think."

"That seems to be a running theme lately." I smiled.

After dinner I signed on to v-chat with Lanie for a few minutes. She told me the research for her article for the _Daily_ was going really well.

"I've been interviewing some coaches, and I'm really getting some good stuff," she said proudly. "Luckily, they don't freak out as much as <u>some people.</u>"

I knew she was talking about the Titans, but I didn't feel like getting into it. And I really hoped her interviews weren't still stirring up trouble. The last thing I needed was more Titan vs. Lanie drama.

"So what's your research showing you?" I asked. <u>"Do</u> the Titans deserve all the Benjamins they get?" I really hope they do. I would hate to be dreaming about being on a team that has some kind of unfair advantage. Even though I've taken a vow to try to care less about what the Titans think, I'm still hoping that this whole

GIVE ME A 103!

Bevan thing just blows over and my chances of one day making the team, however slim, still at least exist.

"I'm not gonna say anything right now," said Lanie mischievously. "I don't want to put you in the middle again. But you'll see when I show you the article."

"All right." I sighed.

I had to keep my convo with her pretty short, though. I have soooo much homework to do, and between memorizing the spirit rules and getting the Grizzlies ready for the Regional Qualifier, I've kind of not been putting 100% into schoolwork. Which, if I were a Titan, would probably get me kicked off the team. I bet people don't realize how much cheerleading and good grades actually go together. Meaning, I have to keep my schoolwork in shape as much as my body. So much stuff to do sometimes, it is kind of overwhelming! And speaking of sound mind and body, it's time for me to catch some zzzzzz's.

GIVE ME A
104!

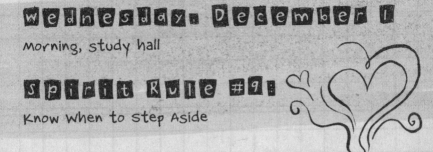

# Wednesday, December 1

Morning, study hall

# Spirit Rule #9:

Know When to Step Aside

OMG to the Nth degree: HUUUUGE news. Katie Parker has a secret crush! I came to school this morning, and as soon as I stepped foot on the school steps, people all around were whispering. At first I thought maybe they were talking about me (weird quirk of mine—guess I always assume the worst). After what Jacqui said yesterday about people possibly talking about Bevan and me, it didn't seem that crazy a thing to assume. So my heart was practically falling out of my chest it was beating so fast—it was so bad that I thought I'd have to transfer schools.

I got my math books out of my locker and booked it to Lanie's locker. Luckily, she

GIVE ME A 105!

was there, painting a red streak into her hair with one of those cool mascara wands.

"Seriously, Lanes, I think I'm losing my mind. Is it just me or is there some big secret going around about me?"

Lanie twisted the top back onto her hair mascara. "Whoa, Madison. Ego much?" She lifted a freshly painted lock of hair to examine it more closely. "Ugh—this stuff never works on my hair," she groaned.

"Lanes! I'm in a crisis here. So, people aren't talking about me and Bevan, right?" I asked hopefully.

"Um, no," said Lanie. "I mean, they might be, but not half as much as they're talking about Katie having a secret crush."

"Katie?" I asked, instantly relieved. T.G.

Lanie slammed her locker shut and we started walking to our classes together.

"Yeah. Apparently she's been hanging out with some hot new guy but won't tell anyone who it is. Tracey Mesnick told me right before you got here."

Tracey is a total gossip queen. She's always up in everyone's grill, collecting rumors and spreading them like wildfire.

"According to Tracey," said Lanie, raising her eyebrow, "Katie won't even tell Clementine or Hilary."

"Whoa, no way. She tells them everything!"

GIVE ME A 106!

"That's the good word," said Lanie. We stood outside her Spanish class for a moment, pondering who the mystery boy could be. "Well, anyway, I'll see you at lunch. Can't keep Senora Hernandez waiting."

"Adios," I said, turning to go to my own class.

Things are definitely getting interesting, and we've barely passed first period! Why such a big secret, though? Maybe the guy is older or from another school?

On my way to Mr. Hobart's class, I passed Katie hanging with some of her teammates. They were some of the more novice cheerleaders on the team—and they looked like they were falling all over Katie to find out if the rumor is true. I couldn't hear exactly what they were asking her, but she seemed to be looking extremely happy with all the attention while she shook her head to their questions. They were all literally dying to know who this crush is, and I can't really blame them.

But all I can think is, "I am so, so, so glad she's crushin', because <u>that</u> means she's hopefully, possibly, maybe over Bevan Ramsey!" I mean, if she has a crush, that means she can't still be dreaming about her ex-bf, right? And that means that it might be ok for me to go out with him again, maybe this time not in secret. Then

GIVE ME A 107!

again, arrggg! Tango uno problem, as Señora Hernandez might say. He hasn't exactly asked me out on another date! I'm starting to think I should be reading those annoying magazines and following the rules about "How to Make a Guy Fall in Love with You from 20 Feet Away" or something. Or maybe I should ask Clementine for advice (yah, right). She always seems to have twelve guys trailing her wherever she goes. MUCHO annoying.

How To Make a Guy Fall In Love With You From 20ft. Away!

YOU Magazine

## LUNCHTIME, SCHOOL CAF

The plot thickened at lunch! Evan was sketching away on his latest comic, so Lanie and I, being, well, us, started bugging him to show it to us.

"It's not ready," he said, squinting down at the pile of pink rubber left from his erasing frenzy a few moments before. Finally just, like, jokingly, I took the comic from under his nose while he went to reach for a bite of his sandwich.

GIVE ME A 108!

"Hey, give it back!" he snapped.

"Just a minute," I said in a singsongy way. When I saw the title and the cover of this latest SuperBoy, it took me a moment to realize this issue looked **VERY** different from the last. **THIS** cover had an image of a beautiful girl wearing oversize sunglasses, leggings, and a long T-shirt belted at the waist. He had drawn her stuffing a cape into her pocketbook. He changed the title to SuperGirl!

Lanie and I read the comic together, and I kept on looking at her like, "Um, are you seeing this?," but she was kind of acting funny about the whole thing.

In this issue, there are two bad guys—a boy and a girl— going nuts in a mall and stealing a whole bunch of stuff from people's bags while they're shopping. "Help! My child's precious Nintendo Wii!" yells one helpless mom. SuperGirl does a quick change behind a clothing rack, disguising herself as a store clerk, and does a ton of gymnastics and cheer-type flips to knock the two thieves out and lock them and their stash into a dressing room. She's waiting for the police to come when the boy evildoer breaks out of the dressing room and whams SuperGirl in the head with a shopping bag full of loot. That's when SuperBoy launches a sneak attack: He comes out of the dressing room next door, where he'd been trying on clothes. He quickly sees what's happening, pins the boy thief—caught unawares—against the wall, and handcuffs him. "What the . . . ?" says the thief. Meanwhile, the girl thief is yelling, "Let me out! Let me out!" Then SuperGirl, all awestruck, shouts, "Who are you?" The comic ends with a "Stay tuned for the next SuperGirl and find out what happens!"

Something about the characters in the strip looked mega familiar. Like, he based them on people I know. It took me a second or two to realize why: The evildoers look a lot (I'm not kidding!) like Bevan and me. And SuperGirl, with her cascading blond hair, the outfit, and even her tiny little beauty mark above her lip, looks like, get this—Katie Parker!!! I think my first thought was, "Who knew Evan could draw girls so well?" Shrug. And then I was like, "Since when did he start looking at Katie Parker long enough to draw her?" I can't tell

GIVE ME A
.110!

what bothers me more—the fact that he took the time to draw Katie, or the fact that she looks so gorgeous as a comic book hero—way better than the thief version of me. Typical! But worst of all? The whole story seems to revolve around Bevan and me being at the mall. Which means the thing I feared most of all is true: someone saw us together, and for some reason, Evan knows about it.

"Very, um . . . interesting," I said with a laugh. I sat in my chair with my arms folded, obviously waiting for an explanation from Evan. But he didn't say ANYTHING. Instead, when I looked at him, he was staring at me with a funny expression on his face. And when he noticed I'd caught him doing it, he quickly brushed the hair out of his face and looked away.

"I told you it wasn't ready for public viewing," he muttered, grabbing the SuperGirl away from me.

I was like, "Whoa, what's with the 'tude?" but I didn't say that out loud. I figured I'd just wait until after he left for class to talk to Lanes about this. Evan seemed to be a closed book on the subject, and now with the funny looks I was getting from him, I knew I couldn't push him to talk about it. I actually couldn't believe Lanie didn't also realize how freaky Evan's drawings were. And I was wondering: "Hello? Why is Lanie being so

GIVE ME A
!!!

quiet all of a sudden?" Lanes never misses a chance to poke at me or Evan when she senses drama.

Finally Evan left, and Lanie and I were alone. "Lanie, I must be going to crazy Town again," I said.

"What do you mean?" Lanie stared down at her plate, pushing around the last bites of the cafeteria's "Fiesta Day" veggie taco.

"I know it might <u>seem</u> like I think the whole world is about me, but I swear, there's something about the girl thief in Evan's story that looks a lot like me—like, totally the way Evan draws me."

I waited for Lanes to say something, but she remained quiet. So I continued telling her my theory: "And the guy thief looks like Bevan. And weirdest of all, SuperGirl is practically Katie Parker's twin! I think the whole SuperGirl story has something to do with me and Bevan being at the mall that day."

More silence.

"What, is everyone giving me the silent treatment now?" I joked, motioning to the empty seats at our table.

"OK." She sighed. "So, before you got to lunch, Evan and I were talking. And I know this is completely crazy and I shouldn't really be telling you, but . . . Evan's kinda been hanging out with Katie lately." She

GIVE ME A 112!

bit her lip, waiting for my response.

*eeeeww!!!* That's when I almost stopped breathing for the second time today. Katie? And Evan? There wasn't a stranger pairing on earth!! Evan and Katie together was, like, a peanut butter and salami sandwich. Like putting pickles in your yogurt. Seriously? No. Way.

"Wait, why wouldn't he tell me?" I waved my hands in the direction of Evan's seat at the table moments before. "And were you even going to tell me? I thought we told each other everything." I was really peeved. How did today end up so weird?

*Yuck!*

*NO!*

Lanie met my eyes, and I could tell she felt bad about keeping the secret from me—even if it had been only for a little more than lunch period.

"Well, you know how you asked me not to tell Evan about you and Bevan?

GIVE ME A
113!

Evan asked me not to say anything about him and Katie. I'm trying to be fair."

"So, does this also mean that Katie knows about Bevan and me?"

Lanie put her hands up in defense. "Seriously, all I know is that Evan told me that he and Katie have been hanging out. Why don't you just ask him? This whole secret thing between the three of us is gonna get old fast."

I am SO confused. What is going on?? Is Katie Parker purposely trying to turn my world upside down??? I need answers, and Evan is going to have to give me some. And soon.

## AFTERNOON BEFORE PRACTICE, LOCKERS

I waited until the last bell of the day rang, when I knew I'd find Evan kneeling on the floor by his bottom locker, getting his books for the night. As I walked up to him, I saw for the first time that there was something different about him. I couldn't put my finger on it, but he looked, well, more confident and happier than usual. But when he saw me approaching, he frowned.

"You shouldn't have grabbed my SuperBoy," he said gravely.

"You mean your Super<u>Girl</u>?" I baited him.

GIVE ME A
114!

"Whatever."

"I didn't realize it was such a big deal," I said. I still don't understand why he was so bothered by what happened in the caf earlier—when I'm the one getting drawn into comic books for the whole school to see. I leaned back against his neighbor's locker, where someone had graffitied a mustache right by the handle. Uh, hello, random? "So, when were you going to tell me you've been hanging out with Katie Parker?"

He sighed heavily. "I knew you'd see the resemblance. And I was going to tell you, but I don't know . . ." He got up from the floor and slung his backpack over one shoulder. "We haven't really been talking a ton lately, and it just felt weird, I guess, to tell you."

I realized with a pang in my heart that it is true—Evan and I haven't been hanging out as much as we used to. And it seems like both of us are acting weird around each other. But why?

He buried his hands deep into the pockets of his vintage blazer. "Look, I know there's tension between you and Katie—especially since you and Bevan hung out."

That was strange—I didn't tell him about Bevan and our mall hangout, and I knew Lanie didn't either. But before I could ask him how he knew, he started explaining how it had all happened. Turns out that

GIVE ME A 115!

Katie had seen Bevan and me at the food court at the mall—like I had feared all along. I can't believe I didn't see her there! (Then again, it is a big food court.) So anyway, she was crying hysterically into her kung pao chicken, and that's when Evan saw her. He'd been at the mall that day buying his mom a birthday present.

"I couldn't stand seeing a girl crying all by herself—and at the food court, no less! A paradise where only good things should happen," Evan explained with a shrug. "And she didn't have a tissue—so I gave her one of my handkerchiefs."

Of course. Evan seems to have multiple handkerchiefs on him at all times. I don't know any other guy who carries those old-fashioned things. Lanie and I always bust his chops about it.

"When she first looked at me, she seemed like she didn't know who I was. But when her eyes went to the handkerchief, she laughed, and was like, 'You're Madison's friend, right?' I guess she'd seen us hanging out. Anyway, we started talking." He smiled just then, probably at the memory of that moment. Gave me the willies, and I **DID NOT** want to think about why.

And ever since that day, apparently, they've been hanging out. It doesn't explain why I was cast as a bad guy (er, girl) in his comic, nor does it cover the tons of other questions I still have going through my mind. I'll have to get to the bottom of those another time.

"So, are you guys going out now?" I asked him, biting my lip. "Are _you_ her secret crush?" I didn't mean for it to come out as snarky as it did.

"Whoa—I've only known her for, like, a week. Calm down." He was trying to act all suave, but there's no way he wasn't secretly flipping out over being Katie Parker's rumored secret crush.

"I'm not calmed up," I said. I HATE when he tells me to calm down. It's just that this whole thing with the two of them doesn't make sense. But I guess it's happening. I didn't feel like being around him anymore at that moment, so I told him I had to run to practice. Which wasn't just an excuse, but I am really glad to be out of there. A good cheer practice will help me work through this whole thing, no prob. Right??

## EVENING, HOME FINALLY!!!

So, when I got to practice, Jared was pouting on the sidelines. "I don't have a roommate for the Regional Qualifier," he said gloomily.

I'd totally forgotten about the roomie situation. The accommodations near Regionals were either a hotel or a local college dorm, and Mom had luckily gotten us

GIVE ME A
117!

the rooms in the dorm. Way cheaper. The girls on our team were easy to pair up, since it was just me, Jacqui, Katarina, and Tabitha Sue. But with Ian and Matt being inseparable, Jared was the odd guy out.

"So? Just bring a sleeping bag and crash with Ian and Matt," I suggested.

Matt was doing a set of one-handed push-ups nearby. "Excuse me?" he said, mid-pushup. "Uh-uh. There is no way we're rooming with him. You've heard him on bus rides. He sings show tunes in his sleep."

"Madonna's <u>Immaculate Collection</u> album is not show tunes!" Jared huffed.

Matt rolled his eyes.

"Hey, tough guy, why don't <u>you</u> try sleeping by yourself in a creepy old dorm?" Jared's voice was getting all wobbly, like he was going to cry.

"C'mon, Jared, we'll all be next door to you," I told him.

Jared flicked his eyes toward Matt and Ian, as if he was making sure they were too busy to listen to what he was about to say. "I don't like sleeping away from home," he said quietly. "I've never even been to a sleepover. And now I don't have anyone to room with." He had the saddest puppy-dog expression on his face. I felt so bad for him that I wanted to curl him up in a blanket and tell him everything would be ok. But babying

GIVE ME A 118!

teammates isn't what a good cheer captain does.

Then, thank goodness, Tabitha Sue spoke up. "It's not a big deal if you want to room with me and Katarina."

"Really?" said Jared. I could literally see the relief wash over his face.

Tabitha Sue looked at Katarina, who didn't look too pleased, but they both nodded anyway. "I mean, if it's ok for us to have coed rooms."

We went up to Mom and asked her if Tabitha Sue and Katarina could room with Jared. She wasn't sure, but she was going to check with everyone's parents and the school, to make sure they were ok with it.

Problem solved, and practice hadn't even begun yet! But I still had a ton of problems, and I wondered when some of those would start getting fixed. But then I thought about how in The Spirit Rules it says that sometimes there are some team problems that have to work themselves out on their own. I'm not all that good at that, I guess. Lately I've been trying to fix everything myself. From Lanie's article to the problems with our team, I can never just let things go. Maybe that's something I should try to do with my problems . . . perhaps they'll just magically fix themselves! Yeah, right.

GIVE ME A
119!

Speaking of letting things solve themselves, after practice I ran into Bevan when I was waiting for Mom. The gym door closed noisily behind him. "Hey," he said. He'd tied his cleats to his backpack, like a lot of the guys on the team. And for some reason, I found it totally endearing.

"Hey," I said, suddenly feeling nervous. It had been a while since we'd talked, so I wasn't feeling relaxed about it. I wondered if the "Know When to Step Aside" rule could apply to guys as well.

"Whachu been up to lately?" he asked. "I haven't seen you in a while." He kicked some pebbles on the sidewalk. I wondered if he was feeling as nervous as I was. . . .

"I don't know," I said. "Just, like, cheer stuff. We had a car wash last weekend, to raise money for Regionals, and then we had a game. If you can call it that," I said, self-consciously.

"A cheerleader car wash?" he said, arching an eyebrow. "I'm sorry I missed that." He laughed.

"Ha-ha." I was glad that we were laughing. "It wasn't that exciting, really. Except these girls drove up and made Ian do a cheer before they would pay him. It was hilarious."

Bevan rolled his eyes. "Now, that I would have liked to see."

GIVE ME A 120!

"You waiting for your ride?" I asked. Duh—of course he was. Why else would he be hanging out in the parking lot? To give free windshield cleanings?

"Yeah, one of my buddies is giving me a ride home. But he's busy primping in the locker room."

"Does he have a date or something?" The minute I said that, I wanted to take it back. The whole dating subject just felt awkward.

"Doubt it. The only date Mike has is with his Xbox."

"Ha. Right." I remembered that his friend Mike was a video game fanatic.

Just then a car honked its horn. We both turned to look—Mike's mom had just pulled up in her minivan.

"Guess that's your cue."

"Yeah." Bevan seemed like he was about to say something else, but then he stopped himself. Then he blurted out, "Speaking of dates . . ."

He had his hands in the pockets of his sweatshirt. He quickly looked behind him as if he wanted to make sure we were alone. I was practically screaming to myself, "ARE YOU GONNA ASK ME OUT?"

Finally he asked: "You busy tomorrow night? Like after practice?"

The heavens are shining down on me!! Yes! Yes! YES! I mean, that's not what I said. "No, I think I'm

GIVE ME A
121!

pretty free," I told him. I tried not to look too excited.

"Excellent," he said. "Maybe we can go get pizza or something?"

"Yeah, that would be cool."

Mike came jogging out of the gym. "Hey, bro," he said to Bevan, "we've gotta bounce. My mom hates it when we're late."

Bevan smiled at me. "Hear that? When 'we're' late?" He made quote marks in the air. "Like I was the one putting gel in my hair for an hour."

Mike threw his bag into the car and scowled at Bevan. "Shut up, dude. You know it takes time to look this good," he said with a smirk.

"Whatever, man."

I laughed at the two of them egging each other on.

Bevan walked backward toward the car. "So, tomorrow. Meet here after practice?"

I nodded. "See you then."

Just as Bevan closed the door behind him, I could hear Mike saying, "Oooh, Bevan, my man. A cheerleader! High five."

I caught a quick glance at Bevan's face when they were driving away, and he looked soooo embarrassed.

Well, at least it's not just me anymore.

Woohoo! A real date! Not just, like, meeting up in

GIVE ME A
122!

the halls or bumping into each other in malls (hey, that rhymes!). We'll actually be hanging out on purpose this time. And I don't feel that worried about it, like wondering if Katie will be mad or not. Because now she has her own little crush (even if it is one of my BFFs). So I figure I should be in the clear to date Bevan if Katie's busy with her own thing. I mean, now that **SHE'S** dating, she can't get mad at Bevan for doing the same thing . . . right?

I mean, Katie knows the rules better than anyone. Sometimes you just have to step aside.

GIVE ME A 123!

The Grizzlies are getting even more excited for
Regionals than Jacqui and I ever thought they'd be.
The squad asked if we could extend practice to work
on tuck jumps and spread eagles so they could show
off at the Regional Qualifier. And seeing how late the
Titans were practicing just made the Grizzlies want to
push harder.

Katarina had the best tuck jump of all, and she
knew it. She kept trying to see how many tuck jumps
she could do in a row.

"Ok, ok, we get it. This is your move," said Matt as
he struggled with his.

"Matt, knees to your stomach, not your butt," said
Jacqui.

Jacqui and I made sure everyone could do at least
three in a row. We wanted to incorporate them into

GIVE ME A
124!

one of the cheers we would do during downtime at the qualifier.

After practice Katarina showed us everything she'd already packed to make sure she was bringing the right stuff. Jared tried to lift the suitcase, but it was sooo heavy. "Wow, what do you have in here, anyway? Ten-pound weights?"

Katarina ignored his comment, picking up a sparkly dress from her many outfits. "Pretty, yes?"

Tabitha Sue ran her fingers along the sequins. "It's beautiful, but I don't think you'll be needing anything that fancy. I read that everyone dresses real casual at these things."

"Yeah, I think we'll just be hanging out after the competition," I agreed.

Katarina scowled at everyone. "I like being my fancy clothes," she huffed. "I never know, right?"

"You mean '_you_ never know,'" Jared pointed out.

"Yes, zat is vat I vas meaning," said Katarina.

Mom walked over to see why we were all gathered around a giant suitcase.

GIVE ME A
125!

"Katarina's worried she hasn't packed enough for one night away," said Tabitha Sue, shaking her head.

"Guys, just so you know what the plan is: We'll be in a gym both days, and at night we'll have a casual dinner. Dress comfortably." She gave a look to Katarina's overstuffed suitcase. Mom never packs more than she needs—even though she always looks magazine perfect. She takes the same small bag everywhere. Me, I need my curling iron, my toiletries, extra clothes in case I don't like what I'm wearing. . . . Sigh. Yet another way that Mom and I couldn't be more different.

my way of packing

VS.

mom's way

Even though I didn't want to disagree with Mom, I thought Katarina had a good point. Better safe than sorry.

"Katarina might be right, you guys," I said in a near whisper after Mom walked away. "We can't go to this competition thinking we know everything about it. We could be thrown for some surprises, you know? And the spirit rules—"

Ian groaned loudly, interrupting me. "All right, Maddy.

GIVE ME A 126!

what do ye old spirit rules say about overpacking?"

"They don't say anything about overpacking, exactly."
I smirked. "But I think it's a good thing in general just
to be ready for anything. On the field or off. Actually,
Mom—I mean Coach—had something happen to her when
she was a cheerleader that totally proves my point."

Ian rolled his eyes at Matt, but I caught it.
Whatever.

"They were at Nationals and had practiced the day
before on the big stage where everyone was supposed
to compete for the final rounds. You know, to get the
lay of the land."

Now I had everyone's attention. They all liked a
good cheerleader suspense story. (I mean, duh, who
wouldn't?)

"And their whole squad was ready—they'd felt the
mat, positioned themselves on it, and could visualize
themselves performing on it the next day. Only, the
next day there was a change of plans. Someone found
an unstable beam or something, and no one could
perform on that stage anymore. They had to do it in a
totally different gym."

"So what happened?" asked Tabitha Sue.

"Oh, well, they won, of course." When Mom was a
Titan, they had a great winning streak at Nationals.

GIVE ME A
127!

"And because of the way the new gym was laid out, their routine looked even better than before, and their tumbles were _way_ higher."

Tabitha Sue breathed a sigh of relief.

"But still, they _could_ have lost because of it. They hadn't even thought of the possibility that it could happen."

"It would have been a much stronger story had they lost," Ian said matter-of-factly, patting me on the shoulder.

"I know," I sighed reluctantly. "But it's the thought that counts!" I shouted at him as he walked away.

When I went to change after practice, I tried to clean up a bit so I'd look good for my "date" with Bevan. Speaking of sparkly dresses, I suddenly realized as I was changing into my favorite jeans and black T-shirt with lace all over the back, that maybe I should have dressed a bit nicer. This was, after all, our first "date-y" date. I looked at myself in the mirror and made sure my hair was sitting just right. A little reddish lip gloss and some long feather earrings I had picked up over the weekend helped make me feel a little fancier.

Bevan was waiting outside on the steps when I came out. He looked so cute! He was wearing a button-down shirt with the sleeves rolled up. I don't think I'd ever

GIVE ME A
128!

seen him in nice clothes after practice. Even when he left practice to go somewhere with his friends, he usually just wore what he'd worn to play soccer. I smiled to myself, thinking he must have put some thought into what he was wearing too. Hurrah!

Good thing Mom had somewhere to go after practice. How embarrassing would **THAT** have been? I haven't told her about Bevan. I just know she would have been like, "Oh, why, you two look nice," and made me feel totally uncomfortable. Maybe I'll tell her if we become an official couple. But ew. Moms and dates? Not a good combo.

We walked a couple of blocks away from school to this really adorable pizza place on Main Street. The kind that makes personal-size pizzas and bakes them in a wood-fired oven. Yum! I was pretty nervous, so I ordered something simple: just a plain sauce, cheese, and basil pie. Bevan was more adventurous and  decided to try the "Pepperocious" pie, which had every kind of pepper on it, including the spicy ones. (Note to self: It's possible he ordered that to impress moi. . . .)

"So, was our speech team any good?" he asked after

GIVE ME A 129!

I told him more about our game this week. We'd both ended up scarfing down our pies and decided to order a dish of ice cream to share.

"Well, there was this one kid who was about to wimp out when he was on the podium," I told him, thinking about poor Chester. "But we did a quick cheer to give him some time to pull himself together. And it seemed to work." I went to put my spoon into the ice cream just when Bevan was putting his spoon in too. "Oops, sorry," I said quickly, pulling my spoon away so he could take his bite.

"No worries," he said, smiling. "You know, I tried out for debate team last year. But I didn't make it."

"You?" I asked, almost choking on my ice cream. "On debate? I'm having trouble picturing this."

"Why? I love reading the newspaper and stuff. So I thought it would be kind of fun. I'm sort of a secret nerd. What, you think I'm just a jock?" He cocked his head to the side, waiting for my answer.

My heart was melting as much as the ice cream. I knew Bevan was a smart guy, but this nerdiness just made him even more adorable. "I don't know . . . wouldn't the soccer guys laugh you off the field?"

Bevan shrugged. "Nah. The guys would be cool with it. At least, I hope so. I wouldn't really want to be

GIVE ME A 130!

friends with people who wouldn't." He motioned to the ice cream with his spoon and pushed the bowl toward me so I could have the last bite. "So, tell me something I don't know about you."

"Well," I said, "I'm pretty obsessed with fashion design. When I'm not cheering, that is. I guess you could say I've been sewing since I could read."

"Cool," he said. "Do you ever sew your own stuff?"

"I used to do it more often," I admitted. "I did just design our new uniforms—and the Titans' new uniforms."

"That's awesome!" he said, and he looked kind of impressed. "They look really good, seriously. The guys were even talking about it."

"Thanks," I said, trying not to blush. "But lately I've just had so much going on with the Grizzlies that I don't have as much time to draw as I'd like."

Bevan nodded. "Yeah, it sucks when you can't do everything. But I'd like to see what you're working on next sometime."

I smiled shyly. "Cool. We should do that. I mean, like, whenever." I didn't want him to think I was pushing for the next date.

Even though I totally was ☺.

GIVE ME A 131!

# Friday, December 3

After practice, locker room

# Spirit Rule #101:

Always Get a Good Night's Sleep Before the Big Day

So, everyone was kinda weird tonight at practice ...
even Mom seemed pretty, well, nervous. I know she'd never
admit it, but I'm betting she's worried about everyone
making a good impression on the judges and even the
other teams at the competition. Oh man, if Regionals is
**THIS** nerve-racking for the Grizzlies and we're not
even competing, I can only **IMAGINE** what it's like for
the Titans. ...

"I know we're just going as spectators," Mom began
at today's practice, "but we're still going in the Grizzly
uniforms and have to represent the team in the best
possible way." She had a hopeful look on her face. "One
day, kids, you never know. It could be us going to that
competition."

We all laughed, because there really was no chance
that that would happen anytime soon, but still, it was

GIVE ME A
132!

a nice thought. Mom lives and breathes for cheer competitions—especially a Regional Qualifier, one of the more important ones of the year. I walked past her room before dinner the other night, and she was watching a video of an old competition, which—believe it or not—actually calms her nerves. Weirdo!

Anyway, at practice we rehearsed all our new moves, like, a million times. Back walkovers, tuck jumps, spread eagles. Jacqui did some drills with the team to practice good posture—especially during toe touches. Which, actually, is one of the hardest jumps for most people on the team.

That was when I noticed that Tabitha Sue had tears in her eyes while we were running through a routine. I left Jacqui with the rest of the group and motioned for Tabitha Sue to come with me. I made sure we were outside the gym, for privacy, and tried to comfort her.

"What's the matter?" I asked.

She wiped her tears with the back of her hand and hesitated before wiping that on her gym clothes. "I'm nervous they're gonna laugh at me."

"Who?" I asked. "The Titans?"

"No." She shook her head and sank down to the floor. "Like, everyone at the qualifier. I'm the worst on

GIVE ME A
133!

this whole team, and we're not even any good!"

Wow. So maybe we've missed one of our own rules here and pushed this whole competition thing a little too far. What if the Grizzlies can't handle the pressure? Jacqui and I need to do a better job of taking the emotional temp of this team—big-time!!!

I kneeled down next to her on the floor. "Hey, listen," I said in the most soothing voice I could muster. "I don't know where you got that idea. You've gotten really good. Your back walkovers are flawless. And a month ago you couldn't even do a back bend!"

She smiled at me but shook her head. "I don't know. I don't feel good. I feel like an impostor every time we go to a game."

I sort of knew the feeling.

"I know it's hard to measure up to teams like the Titans. But we've set our own goals—and we're meeting them. That's something to really be proud of. Jacqui and I are really proud of you guys. And you should be really proud of yourself. People look to you for help all the time during practice."

"Me?" she asked, like I was speaking some alien language.

"Yeah—just tell me one practice when Jared and Katarina weren't hanging all over you. They're always

GIVE ME A 134!

watching you to see how they should act. And you've got the most spirit of anyone. I think that counts more than dancing and what moves you can do."

Tabitha Sue smiled. "That's true. No one cheers as loud as I do."

"Exactly. Like I said, you're a leader."

She wiped her eyes with her fists and then took a deep breath. "I think I'm just antsy about seeing all those girls tomorrow who are, like, amazing at cheer."

"I am too," I admitted. "But we can only do our own personal best. And if we do that, then we've accomplished something."

Tabitha Sue smiled again, shaking her head. "This is why you're captain," she said, getting up from the floor.

As everyone shuffled toward the locker rooms at the end of practice, I shouted after them to get a good night's sleep. "Spirit Rule number <u>one</u> for getting ready for a competition!"

"Does that rule count if we're not the ones competing?" said Matt as he loped away.

GIVE ME A 135!

Jacqui came to my defense. "Just think of it as good practice for the future. Either way, we have a big day tomorrow."

I got dressed in the locker room and was ready before Mom was. So I went back inside the gym to watch the Titans practicing. They'd been rehearsing their big cheer routine all afternoon. It looked INCREDIBLE. Their routine had it all: back handsprings, baskets, double fulls, and standing back tucks. And their dance sequence even had an arabesque double down! They are going to kick butt tomorrow, for sure. I started hooting for them on the sidelines during their routine, but when I did, Katie looked over at me and scowled. Like, seriously, looked angry. And I just don't get it! If she really has this huge crush on Evan, then why is she still acting snotty toward me? This has to stop sometime. I mean, we're going to be together for two days at this competition—if she keeps shooting eye daggers at me, I'll never survive this weekend. GRRR.

## LATER IN THE EVENING, MI CASA

"I'm in!" Lanie squealed into the phone the second I picked it up. I jumped backward onto my bed, grateful for my fluffy down comforter. Every bone in my body

GIVE ME A 136!

is exhausted from this week.

"In where?" I asked. Sometimes Lanie starts conversations as if we'd just stopped talking the minute before, like we have this live BFF wire connecting our every thought so we never have to, like, explain anything.

Lanie sounded breathless, she was so excited. "To the Regional Qualifier! Isn't that awesome? I get to go with you guys and get the behind-the-scenes scoop on the Titans."

I'm totally excited about Lanie coming with us—we've actually never been on a trip together! Still, I AM a teeny little bit worried about the kind of "scoop" she's trying to get . . . but I need to just think positive. "That's awesome, Lanes! This is gonna be so much fun!"

"Mind if I room with you and Jacqs?"

"Of course not!" I answered. "Wait, so, does my mom know already?" It was weird—I'd just been talking to her and she hadn't said a thing.

"Yup, but we didn't want to say anything until we knew for sure I could go. She wanted you to be surprised."

Supersweet of her! Ok, so I know I've been, like, way harsh with my mom for the past few weeks, but she's totally stepped up lately. Getting the Grizzlies to go to Regionals, surprising me with Lanie, letting me take the

GIVE ME A 137!

lead on this spirit rules idea—all completely awesome things to do for me 😊.

When Lanie and I got off the phone, I realized that even though it's gonna be UH-MAZING having Lanie there, I'm not TECHNICALLY going in order to have fun with my BFF—I'm going to study the teams and the cheers and really prepare the Grizzlies for what it means to compete. And judging by today's practice, I'm gonna have my hands full. Not to mention dodging mean stares from Katie, the girl who hates love.

But back to the matter at hand: Right now I'm going to take a break from packing and review some rules for pumping up your team at competitions. I don't want everyone to have the same panic attack Tabitha Sue had. Just imagine if I show up with a busload of cheerleaders with their heads stuck in paper bags because they're hyperventilating! I'd, like, NEVER live that down. So I need to get on that bus tomorrow with a few reassuring things to say to the team. It's our first away event, and we know that the Titans won't be the only competitive team there. Tabitha Sue's worry isn't so out of nowhere. I've read that some teams can get really mean at these things. There was one team last year that put trash in the

GIVE ME A 138!

dorm rooms of the other competing teams. That won't happen to us since we're not competing, but if people are acting like that, who knows what kinds of things they might say when we're practicing our not-so-advanced cheer moves. I need to figure out a way to tell the rest of the squad what I told Tabitha Sue tonight: All that matters is that we cheer at our best possible level.

Right before I got into bed, I got a text from Bevan (Woohoo!):

Had fun last nite. Movie next week?

Yay! Yay! Yay! Ok, so I know that I said I couldn't possibly handle Katie's death stares anymore, but for Bevan? I think I could manage ☺. He's just completely **ADORBS**, and after all my hard work with the Grizzlies and school, I deserve a little fun . . . don't I?

Right after, I got a message from Evan. His call must've gone straight to voice mail for some reason. . . .

"Hey, Mads, it's me. Just wanted to say good luck, I guess, for tomorrow. Have fun."

It was supersweet of him to think of me tonight, but other than tonight's call, I feel like Evan's practically disappeared off the face of the earth. We used to meet up during school and talk practically every night. He's probably too busy hanging out with

GIVE ME A 139!

Katie. Then again, I guess I've been pretty busy too. It just kinda stinks that we can't still be close, even though we both have other stuff—and other people—in our lives. It just feels . . . well . . . **WRONG**.

Great. Now I am **SO** not going to be able to get a good night's sleep tonight. Way to take your own advice, Mads.

# Saturday, December 4

Morning, school parking lot

## Spirit Rule #12:

Confidence Is the Best Stunt You can Master

Wow. Waking up feels like it happened AGES ago. When my cell's alarm went off to its usual Rihanna song, I was so NOT pumped to get out from under my comfy covers. It was still dark out, can you believe?! The only people who get up when it's still dark out are, like, farmers!! I threw ice-cold water on my face to wake myself up (ick!).

I love bed!!!

Mom came padding down the hall. She leaned into the crack of my door. "Knock, knock, Mads! You up? Or do you need the pom-pom wake-up?"

The pom-pom wake-up is when Mom takes my oldest pom-pom and tickles my face with it. But those are on

GIVE ME A 14!!

really bad wake-up days. Luckily, once I remembered the big day we had ahead of us, I was full of adrenaline.

"Thanks, Mom, but I'm up," I shouted from my bathroom.

"All right. I'll be downstairs making coffee."

Of course she was ready to go. She'd probably been up since, like, 4 a.m.

I'd been up late tagging parts of the Spirit Rules book that I thought would help today and, just as I'd thought, could not fall asleep for the life of me. I tried everything: counting sheep, counting back from a thousand, counting pom-poms, counting the number of times Bevan touched my arm on our last date (17!!!), and even picturing myself floating down a slow-moving river. That usually helps with my most sleepless nights, but last night was a D-I-S-A-S-T-E-R and I pretty much just ended up putting Bevan in the boat with me and surrounded us with lily pads and singing frogs.

I got downstairs and poured a giant mug of OJ. T.G.—after drinking that, I finally started to feel more like myself.

"You ready? All packed?" Mom asked as she stirred some milk into what I guessed was her second coffee cup of the morning.

GIVE ME A 142!

I pointed to my bag sitting by the front door. "All packed and ready to go."

When we drove up to school, where the charter bus was waiting for us, I was shocked to see that almost every Titan was already there, sitting in a circle with their bags in the middle.

"Are we late or something?" I asked Mom.

Mom furrowed her brow and looked at her watch. "Nope. We're early. But not as early as the Titans, it seems."

I wondered if they even went home last night. I wouldn't be surprised if Coach Whipley had them practice until the wee hours and then just had them camp out for the rest of the night to build stamina or something.

Mom went to talk to the bus driver about directions to the competition, so I went over to sit with Jacqui. Jacqui had been the first Grizzly on the scene. She was giving the Titans dirty looks in between reading her Us Weekly on the sidewalk.

"You ok there?" I said jokingly as I approached her.

"Yeah," she said, shielding the rays of early morning sun from her eyes as she looked up at me. Jacqui nodded in the direction of the Titans. "Look at them. They're even wearing matching velour sweat suits. New

GIVE ME A 143!

ones. Could they _be_ more annoying?"

I hadn't noticed the Titans' outfits until now. If my hours logged at the mall told me anything, these looked like custom-made Juicy Couture sweat suits. Their drawstring pants said "Titans" on the butt, and their zippered hoodies said "Port Angeles." All their gym bags were silver and sparkly. All that, and these duds were probably just for the bus ride! They had completely separate outfits to wear at the competition itself—Clementine had done a little fashion show with them earlier this week, but **THESE** I hadn't seen. "Whoa," was all I could muster.

"They look like they just stepped out of a cheer catalog," Jacqui huffed.

It was true. On top of their perfect outfits, they were wearing tons of makeup, and their ponytails were completely free of bumps. No one had given us the memo that we were entering a fashion show. I mean, if they had, we would have been prepared.

Well, we would have tried, anyway.

GIVE ME A
144!

We waited on the curb for the rest of the team to join us. Tabitha Sue pulled up a few minutes later with Katarina. Tabitha Sue was wearing her usual ripped jeans and big sweatshirt. Katarina had on stretch pants and UGGs. And Jared, well—he came out of his dad's car sporting the nerdy hipster look, with a superfitted blazer, black-rimmed glasses, and loafers with no socks. (It's not really worth mentioning that Ian and Matt made zero effort for the occasion. I was just lucky they didn't wear their usual muscle-revealing Ts.)

"We would have been better off if we'd asked the team to wear the uniform," I muttered.

"Def," said Jacqui.

Someone tapped me on the back. I whizzed around, and there was Lanie. Yay! I quickly forgot about my annoyance at our outfits.

"Hey, ladies," said Lanie. "Who's up for a round of '900 Bottles'? It's gonna be a long trip." She bounded up the stairs of the bus and then turned around. "Mads. Share a seat with me?"

I had been planning on sitting with Jacqui, but Jaqui gave me a wink. "I'll sit across from you guys." She knows that Lanie's sometimes touchy about me and Jacqui being friends, even though Lanie's totally

GIVE ME A 145!

cool with Jacqui now. Jeez, I really hope this bus ride is mellow. Seeing the Titans this early in the a.m. has totally given me chills. . . .

## MID-MORNING, ON THE BUS

Ok, so all morning I had been waiting for a second bus to pull up—a second one just for the Titans. I figured since they had multiple outfits, why not their own bus, too? I had this image of a sparkly bus with "Titans" written across the side, with built-in refrigerators stocked with vitaminwater and Gatorade and seats that, like, reclined automatically. Seriously, I wouldn't put it past them. Speaking of, Lanie was probably having a field day with the Titans' new outfits. I was sure she was already wondering where they got the money for those.

That's when I saw the Titans lining up to board the bus we were already on! Awkward ☹. I guess they don't always get **BEYOND** special treatment. The problem? I didn't want any of the Titans to hear my speech to my team. I'd been planning to go to the front of the bus and do my thing, but now the thought was intimidating. I had to make do with an old-fashioned team huddle in the back of the bus.

I called everyone to the back of the bus.

GIVE ME A 146!

"Ok, team," I said when everyone was huddled in close. The bus kept rocking and bouncing. I stepped on Jacqui's toe, making her wince. "Ooh, sorry!"

"No pain, no gain, right?" Jacqui smiled.

I made eye contact with each person as I was talking (spirit rule, remember?). "Even though we're not competing, we have something to work for today too. Not just the Titans. We've been practicing a ton, and today is the day we'll show off what we've learned. In front of some of the best cheerleaders in our area. As The Spirit Rules says, confidence is the best stunt you can master."

Everyone in the circle nodded, to my surprise. I definitely expected an eye roll or two.

"You should all be proud of everything you've learned in just under a month. That's huge, people! To learn everything you have in so little time, and being practically all beginners, you guys are amazing."

Ian and Matt did their Quagmire from Family Guy imitation—"Awww right, giggity giggity"—and high-fived each other.

"That's not to say you're perfect or anything," snapped Jaqui. Her eyes were focused on Matt and Ian, and she looked pretty angry. Jacqui's told me she's losing patience with Matt and Ian making

GIVE ME A 147!

annoying comments all the time.

"Whoa, someone woke up on the wrong side of the bed," joked Matt.

"Do you want me to talk to Coach Carolyn?" threatened Jacqui.

Matt and Ian both shook their heads.

"All right, then," said Jacqui. She looked satisfied now that they were cowering.

I decided to continue with my pep talk to cut the tension. "You guys might be nervous about performing in front of all these other squads, but just forget about that. This is not our competition, but it _is_ an opportunity. Today we're going to show them everything we've got. We may not be the best, but we are going to do our personal best. And that's really what matters here today." I looked around me. I think they got what I was saying.

"Yeah, yeah," said Jacqui. She wasn't so good at the mushy stuff. "It's true. We couldn't be more proud. Of all of you."

I think I caught Matt blushing, but I can't be too sure.

Before we got out of our huddle, I led the team in a new cheer we've been practicing recently.

G-R-I-Z-Z-L-Y. STOMP, ROAR, DO IT SOME MORE. GOOOOO, GRIZZLIES!

GIVE ME A 148!

When I went back to my seat, I noticed that Katie had moved to the empty one behind me. Perfect. And totally weird because her whole team was sitting at the front of the bus. What the . . . ?! Now we can't talk about anything without her listening in.

And I can feel Katie pressing her knee into my chair. I just know she's doing this on purpose to annoy me. Whenever I get up to talk to someone, her eyes follow me around the bus. So much for her being distracted by her thing with Evan.

I guess since it's a long bus ride, someone was bound to come up with the idea of a buswide sing-along. Next thing I knew, we were singing a medley of Lady Gaga, Rihanna, Katy Perry, and Taylor Swift. Jared started singing a Colbie Caillat love song, which made even the coolest Titan give in and sing for a bit. It was almost easy to pretend we were just a group of kids—friends, even—off on some chartered-bus adventure. Then Coach Whipley turned around and gave me a nasty look. But I don't care. This is OUR bus too. A little singing never killed anyone.

As soon as we get to Sunset Valley Day, the school where the competition is taking place, the Titans will have to report to check in. The Titans are one of the teams scheduled to compete early on. Sucks for

GIVE ME A 149!

them! Just by being near them, I can feel their anxious energy. It's like a force buzzing all throughout the bus. I feel a little better knowing that even Titans get nervous. They're not superhuman, after all. But I just know they'll qualify for Regionals. They always do. Maybe for the Titans there's never a moment to sit back and be like, "We got this." As much as I would love to compete today, I'm kind of glad to not be a part of all that tension. Us Grizzlies are just here to have fun.

Mostly.

GIVE ME A 150!

## Spirit Rule #13:

A Captain Should Always Set an Example for Her Team

I have never seen so many pom-poms in one place. The gym at Sunset Valley Day is insanely **HUGE**— practically the size of a football field. And it's filled wall to wall with cheerleaders. We squeezed through a team of girls in white and red cheer outfits. "Come on, girls!" one of them shouted. "Get your game faces on!" Everywhere around me was a chorus of shouting, cheering, or clapping, as squads got together wherever they could find space to practice. On top of that was the insanely loud announcer's voice over the speaker. I looked back at my fellow teammates and saw that everyone—except Jacqui (who had been to these many times)—was in the same "OMG" state.

We made our way through the crowds to locate our seats in the audience. It seemed as if all the cheerleaders there had invited their moms, dads,

GIVE ME A
15!!

grandmas, and best friends to the meet. Several spectators were dressed in team colors to support their cheerleaders. Tabitha Sue stuck close to me as we plowed through the masses.

"Wow. It's just like in the movies," she said, craning her neck to look toward the ceiling.

A giant banner hung across almost an entire wall, reading "Welcome to the Spring Valley Regional Qualifier." Underneath hung flags of the school mascots from each competing school. Once we found our seats, Mom told us we should head backstage to the official warm-up area to watch the Titans. She was struggling to be heard among the ridiculously loud noises all around us. "Come on, Grizzlies. I want to see one hundred percent excitement and support coming from you guys when the Titans are out there."

We sat on the mat to watch the Titans as they practiced tumbling. "Point those toes!" barked Coach Whipley as one girl did a handspring into a full. She did it again, this time with perfect form. "Yeah! You got it!" said Katie encouragingly.

Each team member did a few tumbles and jumps across the mat. We cheered so hard on the sidelines I was worried we'd all lose our voices by the end of the day.

"Port Angeles Titans, you have four minutes left

GIVE ME A 152!

to warm up," said one of the staff members for the qualifier. The Titans walked over to their mat to run through their routine once more. Clementine was rubbing her hands together, a tense expression on her face. The second their music came on, they sprang into action. Half the team tumbled across the mat doing various kinds of jumps and twists in midair. The other half started building a pyramid. Katie was hoisted to the top of the pyramid, with a cheerleader on either side of her. She lifted her leg up high to the side of her body, arching just a little to get into a perfect heel-stretch. Katie held the pose, smiling from ear to ear before falling back, letting her teammates catch her before she went up in the air again into a rewind. The team attempted their second pyramid, but this time one of the Titans bobbled a little bit in her cradle.

"Hold it! Straighten out!" barked Coach Whipley. But it was no use. We all gasped as the pyramid crumbled, person by person. Luckily, the bases caught the girl before she fell facedown on the floor. I can't imagine what they felt like just then, knowing that one wrong move could risk their qualifying for Regionals. Marie, the girl who had fallen, shook it off like nothing had happened, and the team went into their dance sequence set to a Beyoncé song.

GIVE ME A 153!

"Nice, Marie!" Mom yelled as we watched them hit every move.

But there wasn't any time for overthinking. Within minutes they would be on the main mat in front of the judges, cheering their hearts out.

After their four minutes of warming up were done, we made our way to our seats. I was basically holding my breath throughout their entire routine. The Titans killed it for the first few stunts, hitting each one. The applause all around us was almost deafening. I squeezed my palms into a fist—feeling totally nervous—as Katie went up in the first pyramid, but she hit it just like she had during the practice. All their stunts were flawless. The girls at the front of the mat did synchronized toe touches while some of the guys performed toe touch fulls. "Get it, Titans!" screamed Coach Whipley. I cupped my hands around my mouth to give a big, enthusiastic holler.

After a few more stunts the Titans began their dance routine, putting everything they had into it. I think for sure they scored high on the "variety" section of the judges' score sheets. It was all looking great, until the bases banded together to load the flyers into another pyramid. That fall during the practice must have gotten to the rest of the team,

GIVE ME A
154!

because even though Marissa Kemper started out in the pyramid solidly enough, she totally messed up her transition from the heel-stretch to the rotation and fell right on her shoulder. The judges would definitely take away points for "Execution." The rest of the team did their best to perform their cheer sequence while she lay there on the floor—probably expecting her to get back up and be fine. "T-I-T-A-N-S!" they yelled, holding banners and cartwheeling across the mat. I saw that Mom had stopped watching the rest of the team and was focusing only on the fallen Marissa. I could tell she was trying to fight the urge to go out on the mat and help her as she struggled to get up. When the Titans were done, it was obvious Marissa was in really bad shape. Coach Whipley had to bring her over to the medics to have her shoulder looked at.

"Wow," said Jacqui. "I hope they don't get cut this early. If they don't advance to the next round, they'll be devastated." We watched Katie, Clementine, and Hilary walk off the mat unhappily. In fact, most of the team looked like they had just been told Santa didn't exist. I didn't blame them—this could have cost them one of the top medals. Or worse—entry into Regionals, period. We followed them back to the practice area.

"Ohmigod!" yelled Katie, her fists clenched at her

GIVE ME A
155!

sides. "We can't go to semifinals without Marissa. She's one of our best flyers. And now we're short a flyer for our routine tomorrow!"

We didn't know the results yet and whether they were even going to get to the next round, but either way, the Titans had a right to freak out. It was obvious that Marissa was hurt too badly to come back and compete. They'd have to figure out a replacement in the meantime. Or they'd have to change their routine for tomorrow—probably into something less impressive.

As if reading my mind, Clementine exclaimed, "We won't win the qualifier with different choreography. We have a winning routine, guys. I'd rather forfeit than perform something that doesn't live up to our standards." She crossed her arms over her chest and looked around for support from her team. Everyone except Katie and Hilary was looking down at their superwhite cheer sneakers in defeat.

We watched them walk a little bit away from us for a group huddle. The Grizzlies were feeling the heat for them. Even Ian and Matt didn't have a snarky thing to say. We weren't the ones competing, but we still felt like something was at stake for us, too. I guess the Grizzlies did have major team spirit—even if it wasn't for our own team.

GIVE ME A 156!

A few minutes later Katie and Clementine were walking toward us. I had no idea why they were walking in our direction—were they actually going to tell us what their decision was? They've never really been buddy-buddy with us—why start now? But instead of talking to the Grizzlies, Katie pointed to Jacqui.

"You. You're going to be our flyer."

Jacqui almost fell off her chair.

"What? Me?" she asked, completely shocked.

Clementine pursed her lips, waiting for Katie to speak up. It didn't seem like this was Clementine's favorite idea. Katie sat down on one of the empty chairs in front of us.

"You were the best flyer we've ever had," said Katie. "No offense to Clem," she said quickly, looking over at her friend. "Jacqs, you could do these moves in your sleep."

Jacqui's face was ash white. I could tell she was freaked about the idea of learning a routine in less than no time and making it look good enough to place in the qualifier. At least, that's what I would have been flipping out about.

"But I haven't practiced those kinds of moves in a while," said Jacqui. Her hands were out in front of her like she was physically trying to push Clementine

GIVE ME A 157!

and Katie away. "I can't just get up there and do those stunts with no practice."

Clementine finally spoke up. "It won't be like that. We'll spend all day today and tomorrow morning teaching you the routine."

"Oh, right. Like you would consider that enough practice if you were in my position," Jacqui huffed. "Listen, I'll have to think about this."

"Thinking won't do anything but freak you out and waste precious time," said Clementine. "Just say yes."

Katie looked at Jacqui imploringly. "It doesn't matter who is doing the flying—you, Marissa, Clementine. We're all in the same position. Remember that feeling, Jacqui? Feeling like no matter what you are—a flyer, a tumbler, a base—we're all in this together?" she pleaded.

Jacqui took a deep breath. "You're right." she nodded. "I remember." She looked over at me, as if waiting for my reaction to all this. I was shocked—maybe even more than Jacqui. I was so used to her being a Grizzly that I had almost forgotten her history with the Titans. And now she had the chance to cheer at a qualifier—and she didn't want it! I hate to admit this, but I'm a little jealous. I wouldn't have thought twice about my answer if Clem and Katie had asked me.

GIVE ME A 158!

While all this was going on, Mom was standing off to the side, talking to one of our phys ed teachers, Mr. Datner, who had come as one of the chaperones. She's actually been hanging out with him a lot today, now that I think about it. I mean, on the bus and when she wasn't with the Grizzlies. What was up with that? I know he's a chaperone and all, but still. Anyway, she must have noticed our little meeting with Katie and Clem, because as soon as they walked away, she came jogging toward us. She took a quick look at Jacqui's shocked face. "Girls, what's going on?" she asked, clearly worried.

Jacqui explained what had happened. "Do you think I did the right thing, Coach? Saying yes?"

"Of course you did, sweetie! This is exactly why we're here. We're supporting the Titans. This is the best possible way to do that. I'm so proud of you."

I had to force myself to smile at Jacqui while Mom gave her an encouraging pat on the back.

"Ok," said Jacqui. "I guess I'll head over to the Titans. I've got some major catching up to do." She laughed. I could tell she just wanted to do the right thing, but she wasn't enjoying this at all. Not like I would have been enjoying it. "Wish me luck," Jacqui said before grabbing her bag and heading toward the squad.

GIVE ME A 159!

"You ok, Madington?" Mom said. She wrinkled her brow with concern. "I know that must have been hard for you."

I was so relieved that I didn't have to explain it to her. That Mom just knew how this would affect me.

"Well, I can't lie. A big part of me wishes it was me they'd picked." It was a good thing the gym was so loud, or someone would have heard my guilty admission. I know I should just be happy for Jacqui—and I am in a lot of ways—but it's still kind of unfair. Jacqui had her time as a Titan. Sure, they were kinda mean to her and all—but they apologized and asked her back and **SHE** said no. Obvs I'm superglad about that because now she's on the Grizzlies, but still, she had her shot. Where's my shot? I've been pushing myself so hard this year so they can see how good I've gotten—that I really am Titan material. But the only attention I'm getting from those girls these days is a bunch of mean looks. I know this is totally cliché and all, but sometimes life is **SO** unfair.

Mom looked at me sympathetically. "I'm sorry, honey. It makes sense that they'd ask their old teammate—since she knows their moves so well. But if Jacqui wasn't here, I'm sure it would be you they'd ask." Her beautiful sea-foam eyes sparkled as she

GIVE ME A 160!

smiled at me. I know she meant it, because I'm good at telling when Mom is feeding me little white lies just to make me feel better. I'm happy she knows my potential, even if the Titans don't.

After all that DRAMS, I realized that our squad hadn't done a single cheer yet, so I told everyone to get up and led the group to a free mat. I'd promised them a chance to show off some new moves at the qualifier, and I wasn't going to let today's craziness get us down. Too bad we had to practice without Jacqui, though.

"Let's do 'Can't Be Beat,'" I instructed. It's a spin on the cheer we did for the speech competition. Then, on my count, we did some tuck jumps and spread eagles. Then Katarina and I tumbled across the mat as the rest of the team started building a pyramid. Ian effortlessly hoisted Katarina to his shoulders while Matt stood behind her, and Jared and Tabitha Sue took either side. I continued to do some handsprings in front of the pyramid. I had to remind myself a million times to smile and look excited during the sequence, but I was so worried about the whole thing that I couldn't keep it up the whole time. When Katarina hit her arabesque on the top of the pyramid, we started with the cheer part. We hit every move

GIVE ME A 16!!

and the formations looked good! Probably for the first time, since, like, ever. Woohoo! Mom had been watching us from the sidelines, and she was smiling from ear to ear.

At least the day wasn't completely awful.

## NIGHTTIME, MY HOTEL ROOM

Jacqui and I just had a little pep talk in our room. Lanie was there too, but she didn't really add anything to our conversation except some louder—than—life snoring. Girlfriend's got some **SERIOUS** sinus issues!! She's had a pretty big day too: she got tons of tapes of interviews and even some comments from judges and teams at other schools. But we hardly saw each other at all, actually.

"I can't believe I'm going to be a Titan again," moaned Jacqui.

"I know—me neither," I said, putting on a positive face for my friend. I can't admit to her that I'm jealous, so I just tried my best to make sure it wasn't obvious. I don't think she noticed.

"The last team I want to be on, and I'm practically being forced to go back there." She rolled her eyes.

"Yeah, but Jacqs, I saw you earlier tonight, and you looked amazing. You learned that routine in, like, five

GIVE ME A 162!

minutes." She has to know she aced all the stunts, even though she wouldn't fully admit it.

Jacqui grabbed a magazine from the nightstand and leafed through it. "I guess you're right," she said. "I haven't trained that hard in a while, but I should be happy that I haven't lost all my skills."

"Look at it this way," I said. "It's for a good cause."

"Oh yeah?" She laughed. "What cause is that?"

"Helping injured cheerleaders?" I tried.

She whacked me playfully with her magazine. "That's a stretch, Mads," said Jacqui. She smiled. "But I appreciate you trying."

"Well, you know what The Spirit Rules would say, right?"

"No, I have absolutely no idea," said Jacqui sarcastically.

"A captain should always set an example for her team. Your team will follow your lead."

"So I practically had no choice in helping them, right?" said Jacqui. "If I didn't say yes, then I would have looked like a bad sport."

I nodded.

"Because honestly, the reason why I didn't want to do it was because it's them. The ones who kicked me off the team in the first place. And then Clementine

GIVE ME A 163!

had the nerve to ask me to help—"

"She's doing what's best for her team," I said, cutting Jacqui off. "I think she's putting all that bad stuff in the past."

"And I should too, huh?"

"Well, at least for now. Until she does something else that sucks," I joked. "Besides, it's only for one competition."

"Yeah, and mark my words," Jacqui said, "it's Clementine, so she'll be back to her old tricks the second she doesn't need me anymore. But until then," she concluded, getting up to go to the bathroom, "just call me a Grizzlan."

"A what?" I asked.

"Grizzlan. Somewhere between a Titan and a Grizzly."

I laughed and went to get my hairbrush so I could sleep in a braid. I wanted some waves for tomorrow.

"Ok, Jacqs. Whatever you say."

If I want to follow my own advice to Jacqui from the rules, I have to get rid of this nasty jealous funk. My team will be able to tell something is wrong—and I don't think I did the best job of hiding my mood today. Even Katarina asked me what was up. Well, she actually asked, "Are you up?" But I knew what she meant. I think what would cheer me up (get it?) tomorrow

GIVE ME A
164!

are two things: practicing with the team (love those endorphins), and talking to Bevan. He always brightens my mood. I didn't get the chance to call him all day. I hope he isn't mad. . . .

GIVE ME A
165!

It's funny to see Jacqui in a Titan uniform after all this time. I hate to admit it, but she looks so good in it, almost like she never left. Of course, it IS a new and improved uniform ☺. Jacqui and all the Titans were crazy nervous about their routine—this was their last chance to impress the judges—and yesterday didn't go so hot.

When Lanes and I woke up this morning, Jacqui was already long gone. The room kind of looked like a war zone: Her makeup was lying out on almost every possible surface; her hairbrush and towel lay on her bed. (Note to self: If the chance ever comes up, don't ask Jacqui to be your roommate ☺.) I can't believe I slept through her waking up and getting ready—I'm usually not such a deep sleeper. The drama of yesterday must have tired me out, I guess.

GIVE ME A 166!

Mom had asked all us Grizzlies to meet in the lobby of the dorm after breakfast so we could walk to Sunset Valley Day together. It wasn't too far from the college, which was good. I was dying to get there and watch the Titans practice.

"What's up with you today?" Lanie asked me as we walked.

I felt better than I did last night about Jacqui getting picked to perform with the Titans, but I still wasn't completely over it. "I don't know," I lied. "Guess I'm just tired, is all." I think I'll tell Lanie about my issue with the Jacqui/Titan thing after the competition is over. I have a feeling that if I tell her while we're still here, I'll start feeling sorry for myself. And that is SO not what I need.

It was game-face time. When we got to the gym and found the Titans, Coach Whipley was shouting at the team. Like, literally, spit-flying-out-of-her-mouth type shouting. Her hands were on her hips, and her neck looked so strained that I thought maybe a vessel would pop.

"You call those toes pointed? Hilary, work it. You can get higher than that." Coach Whipley shook her head in disgust. "I'm sorry, but you guys do not look like you want to win to me!"

GIVE ME A 167!

Everyone was made up hard-core. Like, full-on Lady Gaga-type makeup. The girls had on so much eyeliner that up close it looked like they had raccoon eyes. And everyone had a white bow tied around her perfect ponytail, to go with the red, white, and blue colors of the uniforms. For some reason I had this one random thought: what if the bow comes off during a routine? Would someone trip on it? I didn't have long to wonder about it, though, because my thoughts were interrupted by a high-pitched squeal and applause behind me.

A group of cheerleaders had stopped to watch Jacqui practicing one of her famous stunts: the X out basket toss. Four bases spotted her as she was thrown up high into the air. Right when she reached maximum height, she made an X with her arms and a perfect split, all before tumbling back to her bases.

"Nice job, Jacqs! You got it!" said one of the Titan guys.

GIVE ME A 168!

Jacqui smiled, her face flushed and sweaty. She'd probably been doing this all morning.

"Thanks, guys!" she said excitedly. "One more time?"

As I watched her hit another perfect X out, I realized being jealous is just silly. She's an amazing flyer—and always has been. I've gotten really good—but she's still better by far. To win this competition, the Titans needed someone like her. So, I decided at that moment that I'm not going to think selfish thoughts anymore. I'm just going to be happy for my friend, like I should have been from the start.

"Yeah!" I shouted, clapping when she went up one more time—this time even higher.

My mom came up behind me and tapped my shoulder. "The Grizzlies are restless." I looked back at my team and could tell that as much as they were enjoying watching amazing stunts, they were ready to get their own butts moving. Also, Ian and Matt had started a game of "who can make the ugliest face," which is what they always do when they're extremely bored.

I walked to the team and stood over Ian and Matt, doing my best Coach Whipley impersonation. "Excuse me, but why don't I see any stretching going on here? If we want to practice our new stunts, we'll have to stretch first."

GIVE ME A 169!

Tabitha Sue perked up. "I'll lead if you want me to," she volunteered.

Everyone got into a circle around Tabitha Sue as she led us through our stretch routine. I'm really proud of her—she's getting so confident, really taking on a leadership role.

Jared winced in pain when we stretched out our backs.

"Vat is matter?" said Katarina, looking concerned.

"Those beds," said Jared. "It's like they're made of rocks or something. I should have brought my own pillow at least." He pouted.

"Hey, Jared," teased Matt. "Did you enjoy your little sleepover with the ladies?"

"Yeah, no thanks to you," snapped Jared.

"Guys!" I said before it could get any worse. "Are you with me today or what?"

"With you," everyone said in unison.

"All right. Now let's get to some cheering, ok?" The group lined up, all facing one another except for me. I was the star of this stunt we'd been practicing, called the teddy bear. I did a cartwheel and then, at the end, held my legs straight as the bases caught me. Matt and Ian held my calves, and Tabitha Sue helped to hoist my body up until I was being held in a split.

GIVE ME A 170!

After I was lowered down, the whole squad sprang into toe touches and then made Vs with our arms. Each one of us smiled like we'd just won the lottery. Our choreography went off without a hitch. Yay! And then we ended with our thigh-stand pyramid.

"Woohoo!" said Matt, clapping. "We did it, right, Maddy? I don't think there were any mistakes, right?" He was slightly out of breath.

"Yeah," I said, relieved. "No mistakes. We were all on the same timing." The Grizzlies, for the first time since we'd gotten on that bus the day before, looked pumped.

"Go, Grizzlies!" hooted Mom. She was beaming as she watched us.

"Another one?" I suggested.

I led the Grizzlies in another routine—this time with a chairlift and a back walkover. It was almost perfect, like the other one. Other teams stopped to watch us and gave us thumbs-up signs of approval. I was really surprised. I didn't expect any team to pay attention to us unless we were in the competition. And it was obvious, I think, that we aren't at competition level. But people stood to watch anyway and be supportive, which I guess is what cheerleading is all about. I don't think the judges noticed us, though. But

GIVE ME A 17!!

then again, you never know.

Just when we finished our little routine and were jumping and hugging one another, I heard Katie call my name.

I turned around, and she looked positively ready to pummel me.

Tabitha Sue came up to me to whisper in my ear. "Hey, you need me to get your back?"

I shook my head. I had to handle this on my own. Ever since I saw Evan's comic, I knew that I'd have to face Katie someday. She'd known about Bevan and me since that first day we hung out at the mall—I couldn't imagine what awful things she'd been waiting to say to me.

Katie made her way toward me, her ponytail swinging back and forth almost in perfect timing with Kanye West's "Heartless," which was playing over the loudspeakers.

"All this pretending has been ruining my game," she said. "I'm done. Madison, I know you and Bevan are seeing each other." She wrinkled her nose in disgust.

I could feel my face getting redder and redder. "We—we—we're not really . . ." Seriously, I was stuttering. I guess Bevan isn't the ONLY person I act challenged around.

GIVE ME A 172!

"Oh, please," Katie scoffed. "Everyone knows." She waved her hand around as if everyone at the competition was aware of my crush.

"Katie, it isn't a secret that we've been hanging out, but we're not, like, a couple or anything." It's true! I stopped acting like it was some big secret once I heard that Katie and Evan were a thing.

"Whatever. You're hanging out with him. That's bad enough. I thought you knew the cheerleader rule."

I almost laughed, because hearing her say it out loud—the whole "rule" thing sounded pretty ridiculous. I suddenly had this image of what Katie's rule would look like in The Spirit Rules book.

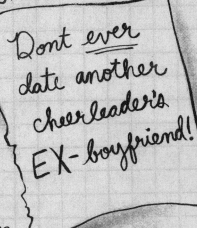

SPIRIT RULE #24

Don't _ever_ date another cheerleader's EX-boyfriend!

But Katie was far from smiling. "If a cheerleader dates someone," she continued, pointing to herself, "that person becomes off-limits. Forever. Even after she breaks up with him. That's just the way it goes."

GIVE ME A 173!

She waited for me to speak.

"I wasn't planning on going out with him," I muttered softly. "It—it just happened."

"Oh, so he <u>forced</u> you to hang out together in the mall that day? You didn't look like you minded," she said, smiling meanly.

I was like, "Whoa." What did she do, follow us around that day? Like a stalker? Freaky.

By now, cheerleaders from both the Titan and Grizzly squads were surrounding us. It was like we were having some kind of showdown, like in the movies. (If this were <u>Bring It On</u>, I wondered which actress would play me. I hoped it was Kirsten Dunst.) Ian, Matt, Jared, Tabitha Sue, Lanie, Jacqui, and Katarina stood behind me, and the Titans were behind Katie. I felt stronger knowing I had my team **LITERALLY** on my side.

"Actually, Katie, Bevan asked me out. And I avoided going out with him <u>because</u> of your rule. Then we happened to bump into each other that day at the mall, and we had a great time. It just kind of happened. We have hung out a

GIVE ME A
174!

couple times since then, but I didn't do it on purpose. I can't help that he likes me and I like him."

Katie rolled her eyes and was about to say something but I cut her off.

"Honestly, Katie, I think that rule is kind of silly. I love the Titans and I love cheerleading, but your rule doesn't have anything to do with the sport. Competitive cheerleading already has enough rules of its own, don't you think?"

I waited for a response. Zilch. Nada. Silence.

So I continued. "I just don't think it's fair that I have to deny my feelings because you dated him once upon a time."

Katie pursed her lips. "You know, Evan told me you didn't care about people's feelings sometimes."

I could hear the gasps of surprise all around us.

"Evan the comic geek?" said Clementine, laughing.

"He's not a geek!" protested Lanie.

Just then the announcer's voice boomed through the gym. "This is the Sunset Valley Regional Qualifier, day two," he said. "Welcome, everyone."

"We're up soon," Clementine said to Katie.

Katie stood there fuming as she looked at me. Hilary and Clementine took her by the arm and led her to the practice mat.

GIVE ME A
175!

The Titans followed Katie and Clementine onto the mat, and I was just left standing there with this look of shock on my face. Seriously, I didn't think we could fit any more drama into this weekend!! I'm officially irritated, but I can't deal with it now because I have to go cheer on Jacqui. But boy oh boy, am I looking forward to that bus ride home now. . . .

## POST-COMPETITION, HOTEL LOBBY

And the drama just continued. . . .

After I shook myself out of my funk, I noticed that Jacqui was standing in front of me looking absolutely terrified. I shook myself to clear my head of the fight, and focused on my teammate.

"What's wrong, Jacqs?"

She shook her head. "I can't go out there. I just saw one of the judges. I—I don't know how I didn't notice before."

"Notice what?" I asked.

"Last year she gave me the lowest marks of my <u>entire</u> cheer life! I was depressed for, like, a month. And now, with her up there, I'm gonna mess everything up for the Titans."

"Oh, Jacqui, no, you won't," I said reassuringly. "You're so great. I'm sure the judge was just having a

GIVE ME A 176!

bad day. You blow half the cheerleaders in this room out of the park."

Jacqui didn't even look like she was hearing me.

"Mads, you have to do it. You know the whole routine. You watched the whole thing."

Me?! Was she completely out of her MIND!!!??? If anyone had asked me yesterday, I definitely would have been thrilled. Even if I'd have to do some stunts I wasn't totally familiar with. I would have just learned them on the fly. But to just go out there without any practice? NUH-UH. Although, it would have been an amazing chance to get the judges to notice me. And also, with this fight with Katie, I'd probably never be invited to be a Titan. It could've been my one and only chance of making it to the qualifier with the Titans.

But Jacqui was the better person for the job. And I'd been an awful co-captain for not wanting what was best for her and for the Titans. The Spirit Rules says you should always support your teammates—no matter what. There's no room for jealousy on a team. And it's true—these bad feelings have only gotten me down when I should've been excited for a Grizzly to compete at the qualifier—even if it meant she'd be a Titan for a while.

I grabbed Jacqui's hands and faced her. "Jacqs.

GIVE ME A 177!

Just go out there and cheer your heart out. Don't think about judges. You're _so_ not like that. Do it for the Grizzlies. Everyone on the squad is behind you. You're an inspiration to them and me."

Jacqui bit her lip. "I don't know . . ."

"Come on, Jacqui," said Matt from a few steps away. "Go show 'em what the Grizzlies are all about." He smiled.

"See?" I said.

She took a deep breath. "OK."

We all went to our seats to watch.

"And now, introducing the Port Angeles Titaaaans!" called the announcer. Everyone ran onto the floor, hollering and whooping. Not a single person on the team was wearing anything less than a megawatt smile. They took their positions right as the cheer medley began.

Sparkle!

"Go, Titans!" Tabitha Sue shouted.

The cheerleaders at the front did a number of backflips across the mat, while the cheerleaders in the back did round-off back handsprings diagonally across. Clementine did a running jump into a basket toss, then tumbled toward the front of the mat, clapping to the

GIVE ME A 178!

beat when she landed. Then there were rewinds into partner stunts. The guys lifted the girls into perfect scorpions, the girls' feet pulled so close to their bodies that they almost didn't look human. Then everyone did some dance choreography with stunts in between while the music played "Pump It" by the Black Eyed Peas. The audience was going nuts. Especially Mom, who was getting red in the face from screaming.

After some cheers, it was time for the grand finale: the pyramid. My eyes stayed glued to Jacqui as I prayed she'd hit it. She launched into her X out basket toss and was hoisted up again into another pyramid. This one was even higher and more complicated than the first: a wolf wall—one of the more difficult pyramids. The flyers held their poses at the top, waving and smiling at the audience. When they tumbled down from the pyramid, the whole gym was yelling for them. The Titans looked ecstatic, jumping up and down and hugging one another when their routine was over. Looking at Katie, you couldn't tell that just moments before, she'd been fighting with someone. This was why she was a Titan. She could get into cheer mode at the drop of a hat. Nothing trumps **CHEER**.

As soon as Jacqui was off the mat, Coach Whipley ran up to her. It looked like the two of them shared a

GIVE ME A 179!

moment. I know that made Jacqui ÜBERHAPPY, and THIS time, I'M happy for her ☺.

Jacqui ran toward us afterward.

"You did it! You rocked that routine!" I said, flinging my arms around her.

Just then Marissa Kemper came up to her. "You were awesome. Thanks for covering for me," she said. Wow. If I was jealous of Jacqui, I couldn't begin to imagine what Marissa was feeling. She was the one who was replaced. At the qualifier.

Both teams waited—without talking much—to hear the results from the godlike announcer's voice.

"The score for the Port Angeles Titans"—he paused— "is 9.34!"

We opened our eyes in surprise. "What does that mean?" someone asked.

"It means we're going to Regionals!" squealed Clementine.

"There are only a few teams left," Coach Whipley pointed out. "And none of them holds a candle to the Titans." She smiled. "I bet we made second place."

For Jacqui's sake (and also, I admit, for getting Katie to NOT want to murder me anymore), I really, really hope Coach Whipley is good at telling the future.

GIVE ME A 180!

On the bus ride home, I went over to Katie to smooth things over. Luckily, the Titans did in fact place second, so Katie is in a **WAY** better mood than before. I wonder if the stress from the competition had something to do with our fight. Either way, I felt weird about how we left things. I couldn't stand to have this issue between us any longer.

I made my way toward the front of the bus, where she was kneeling on her seat, facing backward to talk to Clementine and Hilary.

"Can I sit down?" I asked.

She looked me up and down and then shrugged her shoulders. "I don't own the bus."

When we were seated side by side, I rubbed my sweaty palms along my jeans. "Hey, things got really crazy earlier," I said. "I'm sorry it got to that point."

GIVE ME A
18!!

She looked away from me, out the window. "Yeah, I guess I might have overreacted. Listen, I wish I had known you didn't, like, 'go after' Bevan. I think I would have handled the whole thing better. I thought you did it on purpose or something."

"Well, I have to be honest. I've liked him for a while, even though I wished I didn't. But I did try really hard to stay away from him. I didn't want this to come between, you know, the Titans and the Grizzlies."

"Well, he obviously likes you, too," she said sadly. "I'm really not good with rejection. If you can't tell." She smiled a little.

"But what about Evan?" I asked. "He's awesome. Aren't things working out with you two?"

Katie laughed. "Evan _is_ awesome. But I don't know where you're getting your info—he's not my boyfriend."

"What?" I asked. That was a surprise. "I thought you guys were going out. Isn't he the guy you've been crushing on?"

"No," she said, shaking her head. "I made the whole crush thing up so people wouldn't feel sorry for me when they found out about you and Bevan. I wouldn't have _minded_ if my real crush were Evan." She smiled shyly. "But in case you haven't realized, he's into you too."

I felt like I'd just walked into a glass door—you

GIVE ME A 182!

know the kind you can't really see until your nose is bleeding? "What? What are you talking about?" I croaked.

Katie looked down at her lap. "He was pretty bummed when he saw you with Bevan. I think we kind of came together that day, both being upset about our crushes being with someone else."

There is **NO WAY** this is true. Evan? Nuh-uh. She must be reading into things. I just shook my head and tried to gloss over it. "Ok, now I think <u>you're</u> the one with wrong information. Evan and I have been BFFs for, like, ever."

"Look, that's between you and Evan. But I'm not gonna date someone who is obviously hung up on someone else."

"I really didn't want to hurt you, Katie," I continued, trying to ignore the Evan part of the conversation. "I kind of liked the friendship we were sort of building."

"It's ok," said Katie. "But tell me the truth. Are you and Bevan boyfriend and girlfriend? You can tell me now."

"I honestly don't know what we are." Because, really? I don't.

Katie just nodded. "That's fair." She looked out the window again.

Lanie walked down the aisle toward where Mom was

GIVE ME A 183!

sitting and mouthed to me, "You ok?"

I nodded.

I really want Katie to not be mad at me anymore. It's been making me so sick these past few weeks. But it's up to her now. She'll either forgive me and move on or hold this against me forever. I remembered another good spirit rule: when in doubt, smile it out. "We good?" I asked Katie, putting my hand on her shoulder and smiling.

She turned to face me and smiled. "Yeah, we're good."

I walked back to my seat, breathing out a sigh of relief. That was H-E-A-V-Y. I can't believe how majorly things got out of hand earlier today. All I can think is, **THANK GOD** the day is O-V-E-R.

"So, what happened?" asked Lanie when she came back to our seat.

"Do you mind if I fill you in later? I kind of want to think about things," I said.

"Totally," said Lanes.

I put on my iPod mix and closed my eyes, going over my conversation with Katie. I still was kind of shocked that the tension from the past few weeks was finally over.

Suddenly my phone vibrated with a text message.

GIVE ME A 184!

Guess who it was from?

Bevan: What's up? Haven't heard from u in a while. ☹

Madison: Sorry! Been a craaazy day.

Bevan: When will u be back? Can we c that movie tmrw?

Madison: It's a date.

Yippie!!! That's how I feel at this very moment. And . . . since I was finally allowed to be honest with Katie, it's about time I'm honest with myself. Bevan and I aren't "just" hanging out (right??!) Not when he's always finding reasons to ask me to go somewhere with him. That's gotta mean more than just "hanging." I'm not entirely sure how much more, but more. Definitely.

Yup, this **IS**—without a doubt—a date.

GIVE ME A 185!

## Spirit Rule #16:

When Life Throws You Lemons,
Write a Cheer About It

CHEER!

Tonight we had our first game since coming back
from the qualifier and decided to debut everything
we've learned from The Spirit Rules book, including
some of the routines we did at the qualifier. It was a
swim meet, so we had more room to move around than
we usually do in tiny classrooms. Also, our school swim
team is way more of a "sport" to cheer for than, say,
speech club. So we were psyched.

All day I'd been looking forward to the swim meet.
So when we entered the chlorine-filled room, I was
totally pumped. I could smell the spirit! But I could tell
most of the team was nervous to put all their stunts
together in front of a crowd that was just focused on
them. The qualifier was one thing—we were showing
off while lots of people just happened to be there, but
they weren't there to watch US. There were tons of

GIVE ME A
186!

other WAY better cheerleaders they were watching. This time we were the only ones to watch (oh, and the swim team too 😊).

"Ok, Grizzlies," said Jacqui, "make it count. Don't look afraid. You own these moves."

The team stood at the ready. Jared was going to attempt a chairlift like we'd done at the qualifier, with Katarina as flyer. I caught his eye and winked.

The swim meet was going great—our team was kicking butt.

GET FRESH! GET WET!

PORT ANGELES SWIM TEAM HAS OUR BET!

We cheered, doing some choreography I'd taught the team earlier last week.

Mom gave us the thumbs-up as Jacqui, Katarina, and I went into our first formation. Katarina almost kicked Jared in the face with her shoe, but she stayed up there long enough to lift her arms into a V. Ian and Matt did some back walkovers—being careful not to fall into the pool, of course.

And the whole team did some great toe touches—even Tabitha Sue, who couldn't even touch her toes from a standing position when we first got together in September! We didn't do them at the same time, but hey, we're on our way.

GIVE ME A 187!

In the end, our team won by a huge margin.

Lana Hendrick, the captain of the swim team, is one of the most built girls I've, like, ever seen. I know that cheerleading takes a lot of muscle, but cheerleaders tend to look longer and leaner. Swimmers, wow. They look like they can lift horses. "Nice job!" I said to Lana.

"Hey, you too," she said. "Looks like the Grizzlies have come a long way."

"Thanks!" I beamed. We've never gotten props from other teams before. It was a first. I wanted to take a snapshot of the moment and frame it.

We all sprinted down the hall toward the locker rooms when the meet was over.

"Guess what, Grizzlies?" I said to the squad. "The swim captain and her team think we're the bomb."

The team let go a stream of "Woohoo's," "Awesome's," and "Cool's."

Yep, we are definitely on our way ☺.

GIVE ME A
188!

Later on I went to meet Lanie in the library, where she was working on finishing her article. As the smell of dusty books entered my nose, I remembered I hadn't looked at the due date for the Spirit Rules book in a while. Ugh. Nothing is worse than an overdue library book—if you keep one too long at our school, they make you work student-helper shifts reshelving stinky old books. Gross.

Lanie was sitting in the far corner of the library, where it's unusually dark and where all the real losers in school usually sit. Everyone calls it the "Dark Side" for two reasons: One is because it's always dark (I think there must be a bunch of lights out that no one has bothered replacing), and the other is that once you've been spotted there, people will talk about you like you're a big nerd. I'm not calling Lanie a loser—DUH, she's my BFF. I'm just saying that the kids who hang out on the Dark Side are so afraid of the rest of the world, they literally hide out in the scariest, darkest areas of the library until their parents can pick them up at the end of the day. Most of them aren't even reading or doing work anyway. (As I walked toward Lanie, I noted three separate people playing some sort of role-playing video game on their laptops.) It was

GIVE ME A 189!

a good thing I found her. Sitting in that part of the library is, like, social suicide.

I tapped Lanie on the shoulder and she nearly jumped out of her seat.

"Whoa, you spooked me," she said, her eyes wide.

"Sorry. They really should turn up the music in here," I joked. "Then people might not be so afraid if they're approached from behind. Um, Lanie, why are you sitting on the Dark Side? This place is C-R-E-E-P-Y."

Lanie looked around her as if realizing where she'd been this whole time. She frowned. "Oops. I didn't realize that's where I was. I've been so obsessed with finishing this article, I didn't even look where I was going."

"Well, it is pretty quiet and depressing back here."

"Jeez, Mads," Lanie joked, "what a surprise. Quiet. In a library! Who would have thunk it?"

We both laughed. Lanie is always making fun of me for not being more the studious type. I make fun of her for being a dork sometimes. It's very symbiotic.

Anyway, Lanie had a ton of papers in front of her, all of them marked in red. But one pile was just black type and otherwise completely spotless.

"Here," she said, handing that one to me.

I looked down. The headline read "Who's Flipping Out over Athletic Funding?"

GIVE ME A 190!

So it looked like Lanie had proven what I've been thinking all along. The Titans earn their cash fair and square. I couldn't wait to read it, but then I remembered why she was showing it to me.

And I felt totally guilty.

I handed it back to her, shaking my head. "Lanes, I don't need to read this," I explained. "I trust you that the article is completely fair and that you did your best job as a writer."

Lanie rolled her eyes. "I'm not showing it to you because of that, dork. I know you trust me. I want you to read it because you're my best friend."

Awww! Seriously, I was so touched. And this is why I could never survive without Lanie. She's like . . . the salt to my pepper, the vanilla ice cream to my root beer (mmm . . . delish! Might have to make one of those later), the soup to my spoon ☺.

GIVE ME A 191!

Madison  Bevan

SWAK!

Ready for the really, really good news? Bevan's and my date tonight was AWESOME. I mean, if I could record audio in this journal, I'd be singing the "awesome" in a superhigh operatic voice for emphasis. THAT'S how awesome it was. We went to a stupid movie and laughed our heads off the entire time. I thought the smile would have to be surgically removed from my face. And in the middle of the movie, he went to grab my hand, which I'd been keeping in my lap. I mean, what else do you do with it? If I'd left it on the armrest he would have thought for sure I was, like, begging for him to hold it (which I so OBVS was, but that's beside the point). PLUS, that would have made it übereasy to get caught in a case of mixed messages. Like, say he was shifting and accidentally knocked my arm and I thought he was reaching for me instead—we're talking

GIVE ME A
192!

total and utter embarrassment. But keeping it in my lap meant he had to make, like, a genuine effort to reach over and grab it. Which he totally did ☺. And then he smiled at me.

"Thanks for coming out tonight," he said afterward at the ice cream place near the theater. I didn't care that it was chilly out—I like ice cream any day. Especially when I'm eating it with Bevan.

"Of course," I said. "Why wouldn't I?"

Bevan hesitated and licked his rum raisin cone. "I don't know. I guess I've been worried that you'd just stop speaking to me again. I thought maybe you'd be so hung up on what people thought about us dating—with the whole Katie thing—"

I can't believe that Bevan Ramsey—the coolest guy I know—was worrying about losing little ol' me. "No, I'm so over that," I said, cutting him off. "I'm not going to disappear like the last time. I really like being with you. I'm done with the whole Katie thing."

He raised an eyebrow questioningly. I hadn't told him about my big fight with Katie. "Long story," I said. "But it had a good ending."

"I like stories," said Bevan.

So I told him everything that happened at the qualifier. The face-off between Katie and me, how it

GIVE ME A
193!

almost ruined her competition, and then our talk on the bus.

"She probably just needed to get it out of her system," I explained. "And in the end, she was the bigger person for, like, bringing it up. I would probably have been too shy to go up to her and talk about the tension between the two of us."

"Katie is an in-your-face kinda girl," he said.

"Meaning?" I asked hesitantly.

Bevan sighed heavily. "Let's just say that I prefer the drama-free type." Then he held out his ice cream cone to me and asked, "Wanna kiss?"

My heart started beating superfast. We hadn't kissed yet, and I was dying to . . . but the way he was doing it seemed kinda strange. First of all, I'm not an expert or anything, but I was thinking that the cone would kind of get in the way if he kept holding it there like that. Second, I always imagined that kisses happened romantically and in the moment—not the way he did it like he was asking for a piece of gum or whether or not someone was sitting in the empty seat next to me.

"Uh . . ." was all I could say. Then I took a nervous lick of my cone.

He was still holding his cone out to me. If we were

GIVE ME A 1941!

gonna kiss, I'd have to be careful not to crash into his cone. AWKWARD much?

Suddenly he laughed, apparently realizing what I was thinking. "I meant an ice cream kiss. Here," he said, taking my cone from my hand and mashing it against his. He handed it back to me, rum raisin ice cream now sitting on top of my vanilla chocolate chip.

I took a bite, dying from embarrassment.

And then he leaned into me, brushed a strand of hair out of my face, and said, "Of course, we _could_ do the regular kind too." (I think he may have blushed, too, but no confirmation on that bit.)

Then he leaned forward and kissed me.

Just so there's no confusion, I'm going to go ahead and write that again: BEVAN RAMSEY KISSED ME!!!

CAN YOU BELIEVE???!!!

And now for the bad news: when I came home tonight, Mom was in this really strange mood. She was in the kitchen humming to herself and dancing with a bottle of sparkling wine, her fave. She poured herself a little glass, sighing dreamily.

GIVE ME A 195!

"Oh, Madison," she said as we sat across from each other at the table. She chewed daintily on her steamed asparagus. "Falling in love in school. There's nothing like it."

My mouth went totally dry. Ew, ew, ew. Was she trying to talk to me about Bevan? I'm close to my mom and all, but I don't really need to bond with her over boy stuff.

She randomly launched into this whole story about one of her many boyfriends in high school. "He was a football player, like your dad. But this was before Dad transferred to the school," she said quickly. She went on and on describing him to me. "Sweet, smart, and had a killer bod," she said, then laughed to herself. "No one says that anymore, huh? 'Bod'?"

"No, not really," I said, embarrassed.

Please oh please, I prayed to myself. Please end this conversation now. Awkward!

"Mr. Datner kind of reminds me of him." She sighed.

DOUBLE UGH. It was all making sense now! Mom had been hanging with Mr. Datner every second she wasn't with us at the qualifier. I'd been so busy with my own drama to think much of it. And then they sat together on the way back. Of course, I just thought that's what chaperones on school trips do—hang out

GIVE ME A 196!

and talk. It's not like she was gonna join in on Grizzly gossip.

"What would you think if I went out on a date with Mr. Datner? Would that be ok with you, Madington? Even though he works at the school?"

Grrr. . . . Ok, so this is why parents are so annoying. After all the awesome things she's done for me since, like, birth, and all the UH-MAZING things she's done for the Grizzlies, I couldn't actually say no, could I? Especially after I already got mad at her for having a matching coach jumpsuit and begged her not to get an office at school.

"Yeah, Mom. Whatever, sure."

I mean, I AM glad she's finally going to go out on a date—it's been forever since she's been excited about anyone. And I know that Dad having a girlfriend is hard for her, even though she never says anything to me about it.

But still. Yuck. Mom and Mr. Datner? Talk about the opposite of cool. I can just imagine what it will be like at school, running into the two

GIVE ME A 197!

SO NOT cool.

of them holding hands or something. It's one thing to have your divorced parents date new people. It's another thing to have to be around it all day—like, during school hours.

sheesh. Just when I thought the drama was dying down, life served up another cup o' CRAZY. well, I'll just do what I always do when life drives me nuts. Pick up my pom-poms, jump high into the air, and hope that when I come down, I'll land on my feet. Like it says in The Spirit Rules: When Life Throws You Lemons, Write a Cheer About It!

Oh, and PS—check it, Lanie's ROCKIN' cheer article:

GIVE ME A 198!

# Who's Flipping Out over Athletic Funding? by Lanie Marks

Think all's equal in love and, um, sports? Guess again. When it comes to allocating school funds, some teams get a bigger piece of the pie. You'll probably be surprised to find that the team at Port Angeles that receives the *most* financial support is not football, not basketball, but *cheerleading*. Why? Because the Port Angeles Titans bring home the most medals, rally the most support for the school, and get the best grades of any sports team.

"Our athletic program is one of the best in the state," says school principal Mary Gershon. "We take great pride in the fact that we can provide all athletic teams with the resources they need to succeed." Athletic teams require school funds for a variety of needs: athletic training supplies, uniforms, coach salaries, competitive events, and safety insurance.

Some people feel that while the school is known to give generously to all its sports teams, the Titan cheerleaders have an unfair advantage. Edgar Holland, who does not play a sport at Port Angeles, believes that "the cheerleaders in our school definitely get treated better than kids on other sports teams. They always have new uniforms, they get the most space in the gym, and they never have to do fund-raisers for their events."

Margaret Wilcox, captain of the Port Angeles girls' soccer team, has a similar sentiment: "I don't think cheerleading should even have a section in the yearbook. *Of course* they bring home more medals than we do—they can sign up for as many competitions as they want. It's not like that in soccer. And who's to say the events they compete in are even that hard?"

While competitive cheerleading is still not technically considered a sport in most schools, one look at the Titans at work may lead one to think that should change. This reporter spent several weeks witnessing the Titans at practices, games, and competitions. During practice, the Titans are not only charged with learning new stunts and routines, but they also must run long distances and lift weights in the weight room, like other competitive sports teams at our school. But unlike many sports at Port Angeles, on any given day, a cheerleader is at risk of causing severe damage to his or her health. The maneuvers that they do—which at the very *least* can be described as gymnastic (and should be described as death-defying)—take both emotional and physical tolls on the body.

Cheerleading coach for the Titans, Judith Whipley, shared a chilling story about one of her cheerleaders a few years ago. "She went up from a basket toss and into a rewind but panicked on her way down. Any slight change in a routine can result in injury. In this case, her spotters weren't able to catch her in time, and she broke her arm."

As recently as last week, when the Titans competed to place into Regionals at Sunset Valley's Regional Qualifier, one squad member had to be pulled from competing after she landed on her shoulder during a routine and broke several bones. The Grizzlies—a novice squad—offered up one of their own to take her place: Jacqueline Sawyer, a former member of the Titan squad. The Titans taught Jacqueline the routine in a matter of hours, and when it was their turn to compete in the final round of the competition, the crowd was spellbound as they watched the squad execute motions and jumps that seemed to defy gravity.

One of the judges that day, Michelle Cooper, gushed, "They had the best dance routine of any team here. It's hard to find a team that is so synchronized in their movements and also so creative."

Says Principal Gershon: "It's true, our cheerleaders do receive more funding than the other departments. But it wasn't always this way. The cheerleaders at Port Angeles used to have to spend all their own money, even to pay a coach. This was years ago, but still. No other team had to struggle for recognition like our cheerleading squad. And the administration firmly believes that those sports that win the most games, participate in the most competitions, and show the most school spirit in a given year should, in fact, receive more funds the following year. We're not automatically favorable toward the Titans. If, say, the lacrosse team started filling the awards cabinet with gold medals, we would be happy to switch things up."

Some argue that the school should distribute funds among all the departments equally. But if that was the case, would the football and soccer teams be content to know that they would receive only as much money as the debate team, for example? Before people start knocking down the Port Angeles system for sports funding, they might want to consider the strength of their own team first. Or they might want to ask themselves, "Would I be able to do a full layout twist if my life depended on it?"

I mean, really how can you **NOT** totally love it??!!

oh, BTW, what does Katie mean about Evan being into **ME??!!** This whole week has been **NUTS!!!!** I haven't had time to think about that part of Katie's and my convo. She can't have been right about that—it has to be a misunderstanding or something. Evan liking me as anything more than a friend is pure **MADNESS.** The Evan who makes fun of all my cheers and peppy spirit? The Evan who obsesses over the Titan cheerleaders like it's his job? The Evan who hasn't spoken to me, basically in, like, weeks? Not possible. Note to self: **MUST DISCUSS WITH LANIE FIRST THING TOMORROW!!!**

Because, I mean, Me + E = C—R—A—Z—Y.

GIVE ME A 203!

And now an excerpt from the next book in the series . . .

# Thursday, December 29

Mornin', chowing on breakfast

# Holiday Spirit Level:

It's Beginning to Look a Lot Like Drama

Ugh. I can't believe what just happened! So it's winter break—you know, a time when I'm supposed to be maxin' and relaxin' and just overall vegging out. And that's **EXACTLY** what I planned on doing—well, except for Grizzly practice, but that's fun for me—before The Phone Call. But instead? I'm having a major freak-out session. I mean, I should have guessed. Me? Being drama free? Ha-ha. Fat chance.

Something crazy just happened and I'm so confused about what to do. I was v-chatting a little while ago with Lanie, trying to make plans for later, when Mom knocked on my door.

"It's your dad," she said. "He needs to talk to you about something."

I'd heard the phone ring a few minutes before, but

since Mom didn't scream for me to get it immediately (like she usually does when he calls), I figured it was for her.

"Ooh, must be serious," I thought. Because usually when Dad calls it's just to say hi, or to make me feel guilty about not being the genius daughter he always wanted. And then I was like, PLEASE don't let Dad and his awful girlfriend Beth be engaged.

I didn't want to pick up the phone. I tiptoed toward it extra cautiously, as if Mom was holding out a writhing snake. I could just see it: Beth would make me go shopping with her at the Bridal Barn and pick out an extremely gnarly bridesmaid dress with like, giant poofs for sleeves.

Gross. Finally, I picked up the phone.

"Hey, Mads. You want to go with Beth and me to the Big Apple for the rest of your winter break?" asked Dad.

Phew. Wedding crisis averted. Wait. What? Did he just say, "Big Apple"? As in New York City? This is way better than Dad getting engaged. My brain said, "Heck yeah! When's the next plane?" Now this is something I can get down with: me, all bundled up in my adorbs new winter trench (Christmas prezzie), ice skating under the Rockefeller tree. Eating one of those big New York pretzels . . .

But then I realized all that daydreaming was just a big chunk of brain fog because right after my first thought of, yes please! this annoying thing called Reality hit: Hello! Madison Hays, aren't you supposed to be a serious cheerleader? A C-A-P-T-A-I-N? On what planet are you allowed to miss a whole week of practice—especially during winter break? No one misses practice over break. It's the best time to totally throw yourself into training. No tests to worry about, no homework to do. It's all cheer all the time. Or, in other words: Cheer Heaven.

And when I say no one misses it, I mean not even the Grizzlies. We may not have any major games, but we do have an almost unhealthy amount of commitment to our team. My daydream of a snowy, carriage-ride-filled NYC trip began to dissolve into a puddle.

"So? Maddy? Whaddya say?" asked Dad, interrupting my thoughts.

I flopped down on my bed and sighed. "Oh, sorry, Dad. I was just thinking."

"Oh, so that's what it sounds like when the wheels spin in your head," Dad joked. Har dee har har.

"Um, shouldn't I ask Mom first?" Since she's my coach and all (oh yeah, and also MY MOM) I was pretty sure she'd have an opinion or two about me saying adios to the team to have a week o' fun with Dad.

"I already spoke to her—she wanted me to be the one to tell you, and she thinks you should go. You deserve a break, Madison."

And THAT explains what they were talking about before I got on the phone.

Something is definitely fishy, though. First of all, Dad is always telling me I should be taking all advanced classes at school, plus weekend classes so I can "get ahead of the game." I'm pretty sure his idea of a great winter vacation for me includes math camp or learning Japanese—not frolicking down Broadway. Like, I've never heard him use the words "break" and "Madison" in the same sentence. (Unless he's wishing me good luck on a test, of course. Then he might say, "Break a leg, sweetie!" But that's totally diff.)

And also, what's up with the super-duper last-minute plan? Did he just wake up this morning and say, "Not only would we like to go on a spontaneous trip, but I want to take my daughter, even though we haven't been on vacation together since the time I enrolled her in the Little Tots program in ski school."

On the other hand, what if this is just a convenient way for Dad to ruin my cheerleading career? He's never been the biggest fan of the idea—especially since he had to listen to Mom talk about cheer the whole time they were married. And look how THAT turned out.

"Dad, I've got to think about it. We have a lot planned for this week's Grizzly practice." And we do: The Grizzlies are training for the Washington Get Up and Cheer competition in the spring, and we're supposed to really rev things up this week. I know that the competition isn't the same as going to, say, a regional qualifier. But it's still a big deal for a novice team like us.

Dad got all serious and was like, "Well, it would be a nice opportunity for the two of us to spend time together."

Guilt trip much? I mean, it's true. Dad and I haven't hung out a lot recently (see ref to Tiny Tots Ski School trip). My eyes landed on the framed photo on my dresser of me and Dad on his old bike, with me in one of those baby seats attached to the back.

Guess Dad and I did have some good times way back when.

But then I realized, even if Dad was having a "my little girl" moment, this probably wasn't going to be just a trip for Dad and me alone.

"Dad," I said, "isn't Beth coming too? Having your

girlfriend there isn't exactly just 'father-daughter bonding' time."

"Beth would really like to be your friend, Mads."

Super barf. Yeah, I can just picture Beth and me putting on face masks from the Body Shop and gabbing about boys and crushes. Maybe we'll download an awesome iTunes mix and start a hotel dance party! Ha! That's not happening. Not with "Business Beth." Does she even know **HOW** to vacation?

The trip is planned for Sunday. But luckily, Dad said I could tell him on Friday. Going to do some major soul-searching. Rah, rah, etc.

## AFTER DINNER, IN MY MTV CRIB

It was a good thing I had plans to go to Lanie's this afternoon. I knew she would help me figure out my Big Dilemma. What I didn't realize until I arrived there, though, was that Lanie had some problems of her own: Midget-size pop star problems.

I know, I know. Sounds crazy, but it's true. Lanie's mom answered the door with a grim expression on her face. "She's upstairs," she said to me, shaking her head. "But be prepared. It's bad."

I was like, "Weird. Lanie didn't mention anything being wrong when we were on the phone earlier." From the look on her mom's face, I was half expecting Lanie to be lying on her bed, staring up at the ceiling, like, Exorcist-style, going through one of her what's-the-meaning-of-life existential crises. Now that I think about it, THAT would have been a cheerier scene than what I actually did encounter once I opened her bedroom door.

Her room looked like Dustin Barker had walked in and exploded all over her walls, bed, and dresser. (Sidebar: Dustin Barker is this celebrity whose photo is on the cover of every teen magazine. And in those photos he's always making über-fake kissy faces that have captions above them that read, "Do You Want to Know How to Be His Number One Girl?" or "How to Win Dustin's Everlasting Love." Every time he's shown on TV he's flashing a peace sign. Lame-o.)

At first I thought I was in the wrong room. Because MY Lanie is definitely not that kind of girl. Yeah, I know she's always had a secret crush on him, but I never expected to see a Dustin Barker shrine in her very own room. First of all, Lanie's the last person on earth to like the same guy as everyone else. In the entire time we've been friends I've never seen her glance at a teen magazine or listen to the radio. She'd much rather be reading a used copy of some old fogy's poetry. Also: Lanie doesn't really even do crushes.

And second of all, even when she does like a guy, it's always someone really dark who wears all black and with combat boots and thinks not washing his hair makes a statement about his love of the environment. Like, an emo type.

When Lanes first told me about her obsession with Dustin Barker, I was like, "He's kind of cute for a tiny tot. But really, I don't see the big deal."

"Big deal?" Lanie had said, looking at me like I was wondering what the big deal of say, winning the lottery or breathing air was. She picked up her laptop to show me her Dustin Barker screen saver. "Just look at those kissable lips! That hair!" she swooned. "And whoa, can he dance!"

Ok, fine, so he's got (what everyone considers) "dreamy" hair that always falls down onto his left eye, and a constant smile that says, "Girl, you're the one for me." I know every girl in my school is gaga for him. I guess he's just not my type.

So here's the full extent of the Dustin Barker Damage: she has three different posters of him around her bed, a Dustin Barker scented candle (the label said "experience his essence" on it, which left me feeling icky), and his autobiography (Dustified: An

Autobiography) standing up on her dresser face out like a work of art. Can you believe??

I plopped down on her bed before giving her a dose of Maddy Reality. That's when I noticed the Dustin Barker bedspread. This was serious!

"Lanes, I thought that I was nuts when I fell for Bevan. But I didn't fill my room with his dirty gym socks. This?" I said, pointing to the Barbie-size Dustin Barker doll next to her bed. "This is a tad out of control."

Lanie walked over to the Dustin Barker candle, her long black skirt trailing behind her. "True love is needs no explanations," she said, echoing one of his number one songs. "But there is a reason for all this. I'm getting myself psyched for when I meet him."

"Say what now?" I asked. Since when do teen heartthrobs make door-to-door calls?

She picked up the autobiography and held it to her chest. "He's coming to the Book Worm to do a book signing. You didn't hear about it?"

I shook my head. "Nope. I don't get the Dustin Barker fan club e-mails."

"Well, anyway. I'm going to meet him!" she swooned. "I don't care how many hours I'll have to wait on line. I'm even going to give him a pen to sign with so I can have something he's touched." She had a crazed look in her eyes.

"You've lost it. I'm legitimately worried about your health."

"It's perfectly healthy for a girl to have a celebrity crush. Dr. Drew even said it was 'aspirational.'"

"Okay, now I'm really worried. Lanie Marks does not watch VH1 or MTV. She watches PBS."

"I know, I know," said Lanie. "But I didn't have a choice. How else would I watch the Dustin Barker Little Bit o' Christmas special?" she pleaded.

I couldn't help but laugh. "But that's just it! My Lanie also doesn't like squeaky-clean pop stars."

Lanie sighed, leaning against the giant Powerpuff Girls pillow that has been on her bed since we were four. "Well, maybe this is a part of Lanie you didn't know. Or maybe I'm the new Lanie."

"Whatever you say, Lanes. I'm here for you when he breaks your heart."

"Thank you," said Lanie. "So. Let's talk about you. What's new?"

I told Lanie what the sitch is, hoping she'd help me solve this mess.

"Whoa. That's amazing!" she said, before I even mentioned the dilemma part. "When do you leave?"

"Well, I haven't exactly decided if I'm even going yet," I said. "That's the thing. I don't know if it's a good idea for me to miss Grizzly practice. Or even if I want to be on a vacation with my dad and his girlfriend, you know?"

Lanie rolled her eyes like she was trying to talk sense into a three-year-old and took a seat next to me on the bed. "I'm going to make this easy for you, Mads." Her expression was dead serious. "You're going."

"I am?"

"You don't have a choice! A free trip to New York? Um. Yes, please."

I grabbed Lanie's ratty old teddy bear and played with the loose button on its shirt. "I know! That's what I thought at first," I said. "But then I realized, what kind of example will I be setting for the team about commitment, you know? I've been droning on and on about how we need to make the most of every night's practices, and take as much time as possible to train over break. And now I'm just going to be like, 'Peace out, Grizzlies'?"

Lanie listened patiently. "It's New York, Mads. Fashion capital of the world. Remember 'fashion'? Your favorite thing after cheer and moi, of course. Do I need to remind you?"

"You forgot Bevan," I said. "He's up there too." Sigh. Bevan. I haven't seen him for over a week and I'm having withdrawal.

"Fine, he can share my pedestal," said Lanie. "But no more making fun of my crush. Anyway, I hear you about being a slave for cheerleading and all, but this is a great chance for a fun vacay. And also, since your dad and Beth will want some alone time, they'll probably let you do your own thing a little."

I have to admit I hadn't thought about that before she mentioned it. Being on my own in the city of my dreams? That would be awesome. We'll have to see about that. . . . Dad's usually a strict guy, but then again, I haven't ever hung with him and a serious girlfriend 24/7.

I just hope that the rest of the team agrees with Lanes. I haven't even spoken to Jacqui about it yet. I'm too afraid of her being disappointed with the idea that I'm leaving her alone with the team for a week. Then again, maybe the fact that I'm feeling guilty about it means I've made my decision. . . .

When I got back home from Lanie's, Mom was up watching some black-and-white movie with Marlon Brando in it (he's one of her favorite actors of all time). Even though he is from the age of the dinosaurs,

I guess he was kind of cute back in the day. Maybe teenage girls had posters of him all over their rooms too (if posters even existed back then).

Mom put the movie on pause. "Oh, honey, close the door quickly, please. It's freezing outside!"

Mom is always cold no matter season it is. But she's right—it's colder than usual today.

I opened the kitchen cupboard to grab some Swiss Miss.

"So, have you decided? Are you New York bound?" Mom asked, holding her blanket close to her body with one hand and her mug of tea in the other as she shuffled into the kitchen.

I put up some hot water. "Well, I have pretty much T minus five seconds to decide," I told her. "I want to go. Lanie thinks I should go. Dad thinks I should go, obviously. But I'm worried about the Grizzlies."

She leaned back against the counter next to me. "I know that you were really looking forward to practice this week. But think of all the fun you'll have. We'll all miss you here, but trust me, we'll be fine." She took a sip. "What did Jacqui say about it? Did you talk to her?"

"No, not yet," I said, licking some of the cocoa powder off my hand. "I'm going to catch her first thing before practice tomorrow and let her know what

I'm thinking. If she acts the teeniest bit upset about it, though, I'm not going."

"Madington," Mom said, shaking her head. "You have to make the decision that's right for you. Don't worry about other people so much."

"I know, I know," I muttered.

But still, I'm not convinced. Everything hinges on how Jacqui and the Grizzlies react.

Later on I called Bevan to give him the update too.

"Awesome!" he said, when I told him about the trip. "I remember you saying that you haven't been on a vacation with your fam in a while."

It's true, I did mention that. I just didn't think it would happen so soon. I guess I was picturing something over the summer—but even then, that would interfere with cheer. I can't really win, I guess.

"Yeah, coming from the guy who goes on three big family vacations a year. I knew you'd understand."

This year Bevan has already been to Aruba and Florida, and they've also taken a family ski trip. And the year isn't even over yet, technically.

"I wouldn't consider visiting my grandparents' condo in Florida a vacation," said Bevan.

"Uh, spoiled much? Anywhere with palm trees and sun is a vacation to me."

"Yeah, yeah. Anyway, I'm happy for you. I mean, I'll miss you, but still. You'll have a blast in New York. I'll tell you some places to hit up."

Of course he's already been to New York. Probably, like, ten times.

"Cool. But I'm not 100% positive I'm going yet. I want to see what the team thinks first."

"I guess that makes sense," said Bevan. "The team comes first, right, Mads?" I know he was being sarcastic, but that's pretty much how I really feel.

The team DOES come first. So how can I even consider abandoning them? Stabs of guilt in my side—go away!

Wow, what a day. I have to say the highlight of
it is happening right now: me, a cup of peppermint tea
(so christmas-y!), some Ben Folds on the speakers,
and my journal. Luckily, no one from school is at
the Jumpin' Java right now, so I can just relax. I
hate when people who never talk to me in school try
to chat me up when we see each other somewhere
outside of school. So fake.

Last night I dreamt that my squad was drowning
in a big ocean, and they were all calling for me to
save them. Ian McClusky had sunk right to the
bottom of the ocean because of all his football
muscle. And Tabitha Sue was waving her pom-poms
frantically before she fell underwater too. Jared
did a swan dive before realizing he couldn't swim,
and Katarina was saying, "Help me!" in Russian. I woke

up sweating and realized after a few moments that it was a bad dream. Then I was like, whoa, Captain Obvious—someone's freaking out about leaving the team behind. Couldn't my brain have tried to be a little bit more mysterious and deep? I decided I definitely had to tell the team about my New York plan before my nightmares got worse.

I texted Jacqui right after I woke up to let her know to meet me a couple of minutes before practice in the gym. I've always kind of liked the emptiness of our school over break. It's like you can still hear the echoes of lockers slamming and kids shouting in the hall, long after everyone has left for winter vacations. But today, as I pushed open the heavy doors to the gym, the school felt TOO big and empty. I could hear my heart beating, like—thunka, thunka, thunka. I can't believe I was so nervous just to talk to my friends! But I really was worried that:

a) Everyone would think that I'm not a good captain.

b) Something bad would happen to the team because I wasn't there (hmm, big ego much?).

But one thing at a time. First I had to talk to Jacqui. I know she can totally handle the squad on her own, but me not being there will def mean more work for her. As I walked toward the bleachers on our side of the gym, I decided that if she said my going was ok, I would stay late with her after practice today and come up with a plan for the week for her to do with the squad. And I would owe her big-time, of course.

Jacqui was sitting on the lowest bleacher, digging around in her ginormous bag. "I got you, my pretty!" she said, imitating the Wicked Witch of the West, and holding up a safety pin.

I sat down next to her. "Uh, should I be worried about that pin of yours? Do you want me to take it down? Because you know me, I can seriously kick some safety-pin butt if needed."

And it's true. I know my way around some sewing supplies.

"No." She frowned. "'S ok. Just lost a button on my polo shirt, and I want to keep practice PG-13. Ugh, and I hate this shirt too, but it's the only thing that's clean."

"Here, let me help you with that." I took the pin and performed some of my fashion design magic. When I was done, her shirt was back together and you couldn't see the pin at all.

Jacqui took out a pocket mirror to check it out.

"Nice, Mads, I owe you one! It looks good as new."

"You're welcome," I said. "And . . . speaking of favors, I kind of have a big one to ask you." I rubbed my sweaty palms against my sweatpants as I geared up for her reaction. I told her about Dad asking me to go away with him and how it was super last-minute. "And I completely understand if a whole week alone with the squad is too much to handle. I don't know if I could do it alone either," I said.

I think I was expecting her to be mad, or annoyed. I wouldn't be overjoyed if she sprang a last-minute trip on me, either. But instead, she just patted me on the back and said, "Cool."

"What?" I asked, amazed.

"Seriously?" said Jacqui, smiling. "It is so not a big deal. Don't worry, I got your back."

"Are you sure?" I asked. I couldn't believe it had been that simple. I thought for sure she would need some time to think about it at least.

"It'll be great!" said Jacqui. She rubbed her hands together like an evil villain. "With you gone I can be extra tough on them."

"Are you calling me a softie?" I asked jokingly.

Jacqui smiled coyly. "Only a little. Remember how drill sergeant-y I was when I first got to the team?"

I nodded, thinking back to last September, when Jacqui first joined our team. The squad didn't even know what hit them. I knew how to cheer and dance, but I hadn't been part of a squad before, so pushing others to their limit wasn't really my thing. Jacqui came in and changed that. She taught us all what a real warm-up was—leaving us sweating and in an insane amount of pain when she was through with us. We're in such better shape now. Sometimes I can't believe how far we've come as a team in so little time. Even the Testosterone Twins have learned some coordination.

As if on cue, Ian and Matt came strutting into the gym, wearing practically identical muscle T-shirts and bandannas. Matt whistled at one of the Titan girls, who was practicing her round-off.

Jacqui rolled her eyes. "These guys especially need a little kick in the butt," she said, motioning in Ian and Matt's direction.

I was so relieved. I really am lucky to have Jacqui as a co-captain. I mean, without her this trip wouldn't even be remotely possible. It was only a couple months ago that I was the only captain of the team. And if that were still the case, who would take over if I went away? (Besides Mom,

I mean . . . but that would be totally out of the question.)

Even though Jacqui said she was cool with it, I was still worried about what the squad would say. I told Jacqui I'd tell them at the end of practice. I didn't want to ruin their upbeat mood—they've been doing great all week on this thing Jacqui and I came up with. Inspired by the awesome dance moves from the Titans' routine from the qualifier, we decided to create a routine for the Grizzlies to learn over break that paired the new cheer moves they've learned with lots of dance. Ian and Matt were less than thrilled with having to learn more dance moves, but Jared (of course) was psyched.

Practice began with a few laps around the gym and then some stretching. I had the idea to incorporate a little yoga into our stretches—to really elongate the body. I've taken a bunch of classes with Mom, so it was easy to figure out some basic moves that the squad could handle.

"Tabitha Sue, straighten your leg," I instructed, walking around the mat.

"This is as straight as my leg goes," she said. "And all the blood is rushing to my face. Is that normal?"

"Ummm . . . just breathe it out." That's what my teacher always said anyway.

Jared had already resorted to child's pose, which is the position where you kind of look like you're praying. It's a great position to rest in after a tough pose, but I could tell Jared was just trying to get away with some relaxation during stretching.

"Ahem," I said, my hands on my hips.

"What?" asked Jared innocently.

"Up, Jared," said Jacqui, still in downward dog position.

I heard someone snickering nearby and turned my head: It was Clementine Prescott, wearing just a sports bra and teeny tiny shorts. Somehow she had a deep golden tan, even in winter. "What's this? Yoga for dummies?" she said with a grin.

I tried to ignore her but had a feeling she wouldn't leave unless I acknowledged her presence. "For your information, we're trying something new. Mixing it up. Maybe you guys should try it."

I turned back to the Grizzlies. "Okay, everyone, do your sun salutations."

"Say hi to the sun for me," she sniffed.

"Go back to the mall," said Ian.

As soon as Clementine walked away, Ian got up from the mat. "Hey, everyone," he said. "Guess who I am?" He started prancing across the floor with his hands on his hips and his shirt pulled up, exposing his stomach. He gave his imaginary audience a sexy stare, then shimmied down to the floor into a split (or his version of a split).

"That was a pretty good Clementine imitation," said Tabitha Sue.

"But Clementine would remember to point her toes in that split," said Jacqui.

"I was doing an imitation—not an actual cheer," growled Ian.

"I think Ian likes to dance more than he lets on," said Jared.

"Do not, Twinkle Toes!" barked Ian.

Jared made a face. "Call me names all you want. I'm proud of my dance ability. Speaking of," he said proudly. "I've been DVRing So You Think You Can Dance, and I can basically do all the moves on the show."

"You mean, like the part where the team bows at the end?" quipped Ian.

Jared continued, ignoring Ian. "I was thinking Jacqui and Maddy might want to add some of my moves to our new routine. Watch. And. Learn. Oh, and picture me dancing to something Ke$ha-y."

Before we could look away, Jared did a series of head bobbles and bootie pops, and even attempted to break-dance. It was pretty brutal to watch. I could see Jacqui was trying to hold back giggles.

"Thank you for um . . . that," I said to Jared. "We'll keep some of those moves in mind." Uh . . . yeah, for when we need a good laugh.

"Ok, ok, guys," said Jacqui, clapping her hands together. "Enough playing around. Let's get back to our own routine, shall we?"

Immediately, everyone got into formation. That's something I really love about our team. They know when they've had enough goofing-off time and when it's time to get serious.

Jacqui continued to drive her point home. "You guys say you want to be like the Titans?" she asked. "Well, you can't get there"—she pointed across the gym to where Clementine and Marie were demonstrating advanced basket tosses to the rest of the Titans—"without starting here."

I caught Tabitha Sue staring at them in awe, her eyes glazing over as one of the Titan flyers was propelled upward into a pike, and as she started to fall she went into a toe-touch before landing in a cradle. Then Tabitha Sue seemed to snap back to attention and turned to the rest of the team. "Let's go, guys," she said. "No pain, no gain."

Jacqui and I gave each other a look that said, "We've created a monster—and <u>that</u> is totally awesome."

Which got me thinking I guess the team WILL be just fine without me.

We practiced the routine until our limbs felt like they might come off. Everyone was red in the face from the millions of jumps we'd been practicing. As I bent over my knees to catch my breath, I saw that some of the squad were already heading toward the locker rooms.

"Wait!" I shouted. "I need to ask you guys something." Four heads turned to me at once.

Jacqui just smiled, like what I was about to say was no big deal.

I took a deep breath. "My dad invited me to go to New York with him next week, but I wanted to make sure you'd be okay if—"

"I love ze New York!" squealed Katarina, not letting me complete my sentence. "Ze Big Apple! I always have dreaming of going there. You can go to museum!"

"Oh, Madison, there are so many Broadway shows you have to see! I'll tell you everything you need to know," said Jared.

"I know." I beamed. "So are you guys saying you don't mind if I go?" I asked.

"Are you kidding?" said Tabitha Sue dreamily. "You have to go! Just think of the celebrity sightings."

"There's so much I want to do there," I admitted. "But what I'm really excited about is the fashion." As I thought about it, I started to get even more excited. "It's the home of Vogue! And Fashion Week!" I exclaimed.

"And the Rockettes," said Matt, wiggling his eyebrows suggestively. He closed his eyes and sighed, with a smile. "Ah, the Christmas Leg Spectacular."

"Seriously," said Jacqui. "You have problems. But speaking of legs, none of you are leaving without stretching first. I don't want any injuries while Maddy's gone."

Everyone groaned.

Everyone except me ☺. I was so relieved that

my teammates were cool with my announcement that I could have stretched for hours.

Everyone who I've asked about my going is practically pushing me onto that plane. Hmm . . . either my family and friends really want to get rid of me for a week, or I look like I'm in MAJOR need of a vacation.

Whatever the reason, all signs are pointing to me going. So there. There is no reason NOT to say yes to this trip.

Jacqui and I stayed late as planned to go over what the team will do the week I am gone. The Grizzlies are in for a grisly surprise (get it? Ha-ha.). We planned one day that will be intensely tumbling based, another with tons of jumps (not so diff from today's practice), and another that's going to be an insane amount of dancing. Not to mention the mandatory laps that Jacqui is planning on having them do.

"Don't worry, they'll be fine," she assured me, as I looked over the week's roster.

"Just promise me, if someone passes out, you'll take it down a notch. Ok?"

Jacqui laughed like the Wicked Witch of the West (she was really getting into character today!).

"Just kidding. I know when to lighten up."

"Suuuure you do," I said.

So I finally called Dad to tell him my decision.

"Oh, Madison! That is just delightful news!"

Delightful? Who says that? Eye roll.

"Yeah," I said. "It will be fun."

"Well, thank goodness you said yes, because I have to admit—I've already bought the ticket."

"Daaad!" I whined. "That's a lot of money wasted if I had said no."

"Good thing I had a feeling you'd say yes," he teased. "I'm going to call Beth right now!" I could hear him smiling on the other end of the phone.

Ah, yes. The only bummer part of the equation—a whole week with Beth. Well, as Jacqui says, no pain, no gain, right?

Ok, well, off to Evan's now to tell him the big news. Fingers crossed he takes it as well as everyone else (even though something inside tells me that's not going to happen). . . .

# CUPCAKE DIARIES

Middle school can be hard...
some days you need a cupcake.

Meet Katie, Mia, Emma, and Alexis—together they're the Cupcake Club. Check out their stories wherever books are sold or at your local library!